BOOK 1

AWAKENING
Valkyrie: Alex

BREE KNIGHT

Awakening
©2021 Bree Knight

ISBN: 978-1-66780-999-1
eBook ISBN: 978-1-66781-000-3

CONTENTS

To my husband Ben.

*Without your support of my crazy ideas, this book
would never have happened.*

BOOK I

CHAPTER 1

I look to the sky; as my face starts to get hit by big raindrops and slapped by the wind. To think this was supposed to be a good day for a run, and a day off from work. The forecast said partly cloudy and a small chance of rain.

Well hell no... think again hotshot, instead, I get to be caught in a thunderstorm trying to avoid a demon chasing me.

I am beginning to think it feeds off of thunder and lightning.

He is enjoying himself.

The demon is getting closer, with every strike of lightning I can see his strength building. If he keeps this up, I won't be off from work for long. It seems to follow me wherever I go. When the rumbling of the thunder starts, his eyes shift upward slightly to the sky and then back at me. I will not be on this run alone soon.

The demon's soulless eyes are black pits with a grey glow. He reaches up for the lightning, absorbing it into himself. I can see it in the veins that now light up from the lightning running through them. His body looks to be a black leathery texture, with veins bulging and running up and down his body. He is pulsating with the rhythm of the storm and his power is building just as fast as the storm. All of a sudden, the veins running down his arms light up and shoot the energy at me. I just swerve to the side of the trail.

Man, that was close!

The aftershock of the electric blast makes me stumble onto the ground, momentarily falling to my knees. I jump back into the motion of my run, trying to put distance between us. I feel the gravel from the trail dig into my leggings and the mud splashing my body with every step. My mind begins to wonder, well crap, that is not only going to leave a bruise but may have torn my favorite purple leggings. At least my gin and tonic tank is safe under my black pullover. A girl has to have a weakness. That's some great-looking running gear.

I quickly shake off these thoughts before another rumble could start, but he was gaining again. No idea why this guy was out here. Well, I guess that's not true. It is a great place to catch someone who is running like me. With her headphones on, rock music blaring, and the mind thinking of other things. But, come on, this is supposed to be relaxing. Well.... more relaxing than doing burpees. Ha-ha, yeah burpees were invented by the devil himself if you ask me.

I had to make another dive to the side to avoid the claws. Shit, yep definitely tore the pants this time. He turns back to me for another go but I quickly kick up hitting him in the stomach. As he bends over to protect his stomach, I punch him in the face sending us both to the ground. Mud splashes up into my face mixing with the rain that is already pouring into my eyes. The demon disappears from my sight in-between the lightning booms. At least I did some damage and he might be retreating. Swiping the rain and mud from my face while getting back up.

Mental note; let's not forget trying not to slip in the mud to meet the ground again.

I raced back the way I came, to my parked car by the trailhead. Thinking I have stolen some time, but I get the feeling that it's not enough. I focus on my breathing, trying to calm my racing heart from the adrenaline rush. I know I need to store some energy.

My wings unfold from my back as my fear and control begin to unfurrow, as my fight or flight response is humming. The rain is soaking the usually soft light grey feathers. Feeling like I'm running twice my body weight. The feathers are a beautiful contrast to my wavey raven black hair and green eyes. My face is petite, with a stubborn chin and a small nose. My eyes are a bit too large making me look slightly animated and dorky. There are freckles across my nose which soften the sharper features of my cheekbones. Who said you had to be blond to have fun!

Wings, please stop! This is not the time to fly away or fight from the sky. Which I should maybe get better at someday. Might save my life or at least make me harder to kill.

Damn, he is back up and coming for me again? Why isn't the Patrol out today? Taking a break just like I am trying with a quick run. Just because it's raining doesn't mean these demon bastards aren't out today.

Well, I guess I start early today......and, of course, don't get paid for this one.

I feel the hair on the back of my neck stand on end. Turning around pulling my dagger from the sheath attached to my thigh and the dagger slips from my wet grip. I quickly called the blade back to me. "Veni!" I yelled out of exasperation and need. The blade quickly came back up from the ground. I quickly caught it by the hilt; turning the blade inward along the arm for close-up fighting.

His fist came across aiming for my face. His cruel mouth peeled back over jagged teeth into a roar. I flung my arm up to block while dropping the blade into my left hand to go for the gut. As my blade swiped across his gut, spilling his blood and intestines to the ground.

I forgot to move out of the way of the spray. "Crap!"

The feeling of warm blood on my face made me gag a little but I was able to swallow it down and then go for the kill shot of slashing his throat. Gross but it was always effective in making sure they go back to hell where they belong.

I pull my wings back into myself as the adrenaline slows down. Breathing in and out I try to assess the damage. Well, I guess not dying is a good outcome. Shrugging I step away from the demon.

The demon fell to the side thankfully. No worries about cleaning up with demons though. They slowly just turn to ash and then wake back up in hell. Whoever let him out was going to be mad. It was expensive to get the spell and ingredients to summon a demon.... Not to mention illegal.

Those who practiced the dark arts weren't always bad people, but sometimes they go too far and that's when they get into trouble. The Patrol were the ones who usually took them to Scuro Hall for judgment and then to Morte Jail.

To end up there is certain death.

People don't get out of there easily and if they do they are never the same. I have seen a few of those who went away for a short sentence that came out with their gifts not being intact anymore. They just wander around until they die. I don't know how this is possible. To do this to a person is like removing the person's soul. For our gifts, makeup is part of our soul.

And... there is a shiver up my spine.... ahhh nope, not going there.

I slowly get up, reach for my phone. Thank the Gods it didn't fall out of the side pocket of my leggings. It may be a little wet and getting wetter by the second due to the wonderful downpour. I pulled up the camera to snap a few pictures and waited for the demon to turn to ash.

This could take a few minutes, so I walked over to lean against a tree by some bushes. Using the leaves from the bush I scraped some of the mud/blood from my face and hands. After looking at my clothes I knew they were going to be fun to clean later. Groaning, I strip off my pullover and ball it up. I realize there is a puddle near me that I can kind of rinse some of the mud and blood out.

Bending over I could feel my knees protest from the cuts.

Ouch, yep that will take a couple of hours to heal.

Supernatural healing was pretty quick. Our cells could regenerate and repair the damage that is done to our bodies. Well, most damage, you lose enough blood or get decapitated by someone, then there is no coming back.

Thankfully the puddle was deep enough to get some of the mud and blood out. After splashing some of the puddle water on my knees to get a better look at them.

"Crap that hurts! Ahhhh!" I jump around a little to shake off the pain.

Turning my head to get a better look at the cuts; I get a glimpse of something around the demon's neck. I quickly spring up and run over to him to see what it was. The shiny pendant was on a leather strap around his neck.

His body was now quickly turning to ash so it was now or never to get it. I grabbed the necklace, taking my blade out and slicing through the leather to free it. Then sticking it in my pocket to look at later.

I jogged over to my car for a cylinder to collect some of the ash for proof. Sometimes the pictures were good enough but other times it's good to have some of the demons to hand over to see if they can get a read on who summoned him.

I collected some of the ash before it started to disappear and of course, the rain was not helping with this task. What I was able to collect was so mushy and disintegrated I don't think it would do much good. Getting up again, I jogged back over to my car to call the Patrol. My friends will just have to wait.

Shrugging, I think that at least the excuse will be valid.

My car was a welcoming cocoon from the rain. The only downfall was I didn't have something to cover my leather seats. Shaking my head, I rolled my eyes at this.

I almost get my ass fried but I am more worried about my leather seats. In a car that my friends would call an everyday driver or grandma's car, not like Tori's mustang that is her baby.

I turned on the car for some warmth even though it barely could reach through my naturally cold skin and calm my nerves before calling

The Patrol. I leaned back to just breathe. I began dialing 777 for The Patrol. God, just hearing the ring waiting for them to pick up was hard on the nerves.

Finally, they picked up; a man with a gravelly, deep voice answered "Hello this is Lucas what is the problem." Wow-what a voice I hope the man on the other end lived up to. As my mind wandered a bit his voice came back again over the line. "Is anyone there? What is wrong?" said Lucas. I snapped out of it to finally answer. "Yeah, sorry I'm here, I just killed a demon at Carson Park. He came out of nowhere and started chasing me. Firing lighting at me. I think he created the lightning because it is still raining but now there is no lightning." I know at this point I am starting to ramble but I'm just so high from the adrenaline I can't help myself. Thank the Gods Lucas interrupted at this point. "Ok. Wow, please calm down; wherein Carson Park, are you? " I took a breath before saying "Yes; sorry I'm at the main trail in my car. It's a black Malibu."

To think I'm clumsy is an understatement. It looks like I tried to go for a run on the trail instead of on the pavement. It's laughable really. I have tripped on a flat surface more than once and even ran into a wall a time or two.

That I swear jumped in front of me last time.

Ok, let the brain slow down and stop freaking out, you can do this.

Well, thankfully Lucas took it from there and started to give me instructions to stop my mind from babbling. His sexy voice came through the line saying. "I want you to stay in your car and lock the doors until I get there. Can you do this?" That voice could make any girl or guy do what he asks I bet. I'm not one to bet but on this, I would. Shit, I finally respond.: "Yes, yeah of course." Lucas' response is calm to mine. "That's good. Thank you. I will be there in 5 minutes. I'm not that far away from Carson Park."

A few minutes later a car pulled into the lot by me with a guy that was presumed to be this Lucas guy. I hope this is him. Not only is this guy cute but I am just realizing the time and I have to get back to my friends.

They will be getting up soon and they tend to worry.

Watching this man unfold from the black Audi is like witnessing a God step forth from the heavens. My mouth immediately started to water at the sight of him.

I couldn't help my eyes from roaming.

His dark midnight hair was long swept back from his face. It almost touched his massive shoulders, which I think are made from rock. Looking at the rest of him unfolding from the car I realized he was tall, maybe 6'4". He turned towards my car and I got a better look at the rest of the Viking coming towards me. His black t-shirt was visible under the matching black leather jacket. The jeans fit over muscular legs that could squat a whole football team. The swagger that came from those legs spoke volumes about this man.

He was definitely at ease with himself and knew what he was doing.

As he got closer, I could see the hard-set face with a night's stubble that only added to his sex appeal. His eyes were assessing everything around him. With a last look at his surroundings, he took the last few steps to my car to knock on the window. He moved aside his jacket just enough that I could see that the t-shirt did little to hide the 6-pack underneath. Truthfully, I then tried to get a better look at what was under the jacket, but with the rain still coming down he didn't move it enough to get that better look. Well, at least it was only sprinkling at this point. I regretted having to get out of my car into the wet air.

Leaning my head back against the headrest I take a deep breath. My whole body may be wet but thankfully cold doesn't bug me much. I hate being this soaking wet and wearing my clothes. It is the equivalent of nails on the chalkboard.

Reaching for the handle, I try not to look directly into his eyes.

I open my car door just enough to get out and not hit the man standing there waiting for my wet ass to get moving.

With my clothes sticking to my body showing off every curve was making this even worse. I could feel his eyes assessing me as I did him. With my attire showing way more than I wanted to show.

This wasn't fair, why can't I be wearing baggy pants and a sweatshirt.

The mud and blood on my clothes were not something that a girl should ever have to wear in front of anyone, let alone this God-like man that is outside my car.

Well, I guess *suck it up* is a good phrase for today.

After shutting the car door, I cross my arms in front to try to keep something out of his view. I looked the investigator up and down once more before saying "Hi, I talked to you on the phone. My name is Alex." Before I could say anything else, he interjected "Yes, I gathered that. I'm Lucas Storm" His eyes flash to a steel blue, with a cocky half-smile that was there one moment and gone the next. Almost like it was never there. His face returned to a firm, tense frown that continued to assess the surrounding woods. His gaze fell to the darkened earth near the trailhead.

"You called about a demon attack?" Lucas asked with a head nodding towards the darkened ground. "Yes, I was just going to go for a run when out of the brush this demon came running at me. I have a picture on my phone of the demon and some of the ash from the body." I said while pulling out my phone to pull them up. It popped right up as Lucas reached for my phone to take a closer look. His head bent over the phone giving his chiseled face some shadows that deepened his looks making him appear dangerous. He started to scroll through the pictures but I could tell he went too far because there was another slight smirk.

Crap, which picture had he seen. I hope it wasn't from when my friends decided to take me out. That was a crazy night that I really shouldn't still have proof from.

That night will go down as the drunken night from hell. Can't believe they convinced me to dance on the table at the club. Ok, as an adult you should never play truth or dare. Especially when you have had mojitos mixed by Brian.

That man sure knows how to make a good cocktail.

Well, good but deadly one that if you have more than 3 will result in dancing on the table for a dare. Yep, I really need to get that phone back. I try to swipe it back, but he moves a step back suddenly to avoid me. Then takes out his phone and places it on the back of mine. Oh, clever, he instantly transferred the pictures to his phone.

I hope he only took the demon photos.

He offered my phone back to me while slipping his phone back into his jacket pocket. "You said that you also took some ash? I will need that along with some of that blood off of your clothes. I presume some of that is not yours." He stated while looking me up and down. "I will also need to know why you are here so early this morning in this weather." His deep voice was making it hard to concentrate on the words coming out of his mouth. That mouth had a cockiness to it that had me taking a step back. Which had me bumping into my car door and startling me to jump back forward. He reached forward to catch me. The instant he grabbed my arm to steady me I could feel a vision coming.

The vision sucked me in, taking me this time backward in time. I looked around in the vision and found that the surroundings were of a ship on the dock of some kind. The sky was black with the ocean mimicking it into the night. There were people moving crates onto the ship.

Wow, this was no ordinary ship.

The ship is a Viking due to the shape of the boat. I could hear the men talking to each other. So, I got closer to them all while keeping my gaze on the dock because let's face it, I would trip otherwise.

Thankfully they can't see me in my vision but I also can't interact to ask them questions. One with a grey beard starts to lift a crate but stops to talk to another man who is dressed in ruff clothes of brown cloth. He yells out "Sven, I will need thine help with this crate. No! Leave the rope there for now. I will help you with it after you help me move the crate onto the ship." Sven threw the rope aside and came down off the ship to help lift the crate to two other men dressed similarly.

They were all younger than the man with the beard and looked to be waiting for his instructions.

After lifting the crate by pulling on a rope together, Sven and the bearded man started to walk up the gangplank onto the ship. I heard a yell from the darker-haired man on board. "Behind you Sven! Godrick! Something is coming. In God's name, what is that!" We all turn to see twenty demons running out to the dock with a man following them close behind. The demons are of the same species that I killed today. They were lit up from the veins that ran up and down their bodies. Grey hair flowing behind their heads with two short horns coming through. That's when

I heard the thunder and lightning startup. The lightning struck out but the demons reached up absorbing it. I could see the power of the lightning flowing through their veins. Then they fired bolts of lightning at us. I instinctively jumped behind a crate.

I don't care that they can't see me; instinct is instinct.

Looking out from the crate, I saw them gearing up for another bolt of lightning that was sure to come after the thunder that I just heard. The man behind them just kept walking at a pace that was one of leisure and dominance. He was a tall man in a black cloak flowing behind him. I somehow locked eyes with him. His hand raises suddenly joining his demons he swipes to the side and the crate suddenly gets flung into the side of the ship. Breaking apart next to me, I fall to the ground covering my head. How is this possible? This man shouldn't be able to see me?

The demons are now charged up from another lightning bolt but they were on the dock running towards the four men. The men run to get their weapons, but it is too late as they are overtaken by the demons.

Sven is the first to fall; by having a bolt of lightning pierce him directly in the heart, lighting him up before another demon sliced a clawed hand across his gut. The next three were not spared either for they were slaughtered by the demons. Godrick had a demon leap on him and snap his neck. While his men on board were overtaken by five of the demons tearing at their skin with claws that glinted in the lightning. I tried not to gag at the gruesome scene, but I was barely able to swallow the bile rolling up my throat and look up to see the man coming the rest of the way to the dock. He looked at me again but it was hard to make out his features from this far away especially with that cloak covering his head and body. His hand appeared again and the tattoo that covered it was of a skeleton. He raised his hand to point in my direction but no he can't now I'm here, this is a vision. Skeleton guy then said "Come here!" in a command that was one of death. Some of the demons started to come my way, finally taking notice of me.

I scrabble back.

The vision slowly started to fade around me, but the last thing I heard was from the skeleton guy yelling "No, I need her"....

CHAPTER 2

I came back to the world......my eyes slowly went from bleary to focusing sharply on the face above me. The face I couldn't place just yet for I am waiting for the rest of my body to catch up to where I was now. For a vision, this one was a doozy. I finally was able to fully focus on the face above me. The hard-sent eyes with a hint of worry and a crease down the middle of his brow. The mouth was slightly pursed with the same worry. The lips look so soft I wanted to reach up and taste them to see if they tasted as good as they looked.

Well shit, that was not a good thought about someone you just met and was now cradling you in his arms like you weighed nothing.

I tried to sit up but instead, he swung me up to sit on the hood of my car while still holding my shoulders. He looked into my face again. "Are you all right?" he asks me in a smooth voice as if a girl who appears to have fainted does this all the time around him. I finally push his hands off of me but it feels wrong without them there. I feel the pull to put them back.

Hmmm, that's a new one for me. Never thought a guy's touch would affect me like that but still, I already miss his touch.

Looking up at him I say "Yes, I'm fine. That sometimes happens when I have a big vision. Normally I can be present here as well as being in the future or past. This time it felt different." Not true but he didn't need to know this. Yep, I need to stop talking about this with him. I mean I just met him. I need to get to my friends, to tell them what I saw, and hopefully realized can figure out what it was.

"So, your gift is visions of the past and future? What did you see? Does it pertain to what happened here today?" He asks with an insistent look. I answer back "Yes, it is one of my gifts, but I need to work through what I saw and don't know if it is linked to this or not." God, I hope he believed that last part.

He walks away from me to the ash that is slowly getting muckier due to the drizzle. I shiver again now that I am not in his arms. The short walk to where he is taking his pictures and examining the ground. He quickly got up from the ground and started asking "So can you tell me why this demon chose you to run after today?"

"I don't know why he chose me!" saying louder than I meant to. "Look, I had this great idea to go for a run this morning because I couldn't sleep." Throwing my hands up I continue with my small freak out. "Yes! I know the forecast said there was a slight chance of rain but it looked like it would hold off till at least noon. So, I drove over to the parking trail to try out this type of running instead of running through the city on the pavement. It was just starting to rain and I was thinking of going back to the car. But this big demon came crashing out of the brush and started to run towards me." I took a deep breath to center myself just like my friend Tori had taught me.

To think I was using yoga at a time like this. All I wanted to do was get home and take a shower. Picking at the hem of my tank trying to get it to not stick to me as much.

Lucas didn't even waver from his stern look at my outburst. "Are you done shouting at me? Maybe I can rephrase this so you don't start yelling again. Have you seen this type of demon before?" His voice is smoother with a slight edge that he is holding back his temper.

I wanted to get out of there to find out what that vision was all about and I didn't know if my temper would trigger the ice that is slowly flowing through my veins. This gift was one I was still getting a handle on. Man, I need to practice that one more often, it would have come in handy against the demon. I am a hunter with my friends Tori and Cloe but I still need some work.

To move this along, so I could leave, I did more of the yoga breathing. "The demon had black leathery skin with veins running down his body that lit up from the lightning when he absorbed it. He had long dark grey hair with two short horns coming out of his head towards the front. His eyes were grey that slowly turned black around the edge. Large muscles on a 7-foot frame at the very least. I was able to use my dagger to stop him." I didn't want to tell him about the strange pendant I found or the fact that I had just seen this demon in my vision.

Some things just needed to be kept to myself until I spoke to my friends. It was just the three of us but we were tight.

I re-crossed my arms over my chest to rub my arms out of nervousness but it was no good. He noticed my movement but didn't say anything, thank the Gods. "Thanks for the description and I think that I should take you to the hospital to get those cuts healed. You can also process that vision you had. I'm pretty sure that it had to do with what happened today."

Hearing this from him. Hits me like a ton of bricks. Making me take a step back.

Should I tell him what the vision showed me?

Should I tell him about the pendant?

Should I tell him that I'm a hunter?.....wow, yeah, these are the many questions that need to be discussed with my friends first.

So, finally, I say "Thanks for offering me a ride to the hospital but I have a friend who can heal me. She lives in the same apartment building as me." Waiting for a beat, I had to think about the last question of the vision. "And I don't share my visions with just anyone. If I think it will be helpful, I'll call the Office of Patrol and leave a message for you." At this, I am backing away without trying to look like I am going to bolt like a scared chicken. I turn to leave but his hand snags out to grab my arm. His grip is firm on my wrist. With a gentle tug, I am crushed to a wall of pure muscle. The smooth getaway was ruined.

He smells of the forest with a hint of the musk of the rain.

In his close-up muscular arms, I can see that his skin is pale like alabaster, which is a big contrast to his black hair and bright steel blue eyes. His lips are even fuller up close and when they part, I can see just a little of the pearly white fangs.

Shit! Yep, I need to get away from those fangs.

I try to push him back by placing my hands on his chest but instead, I just rest them there and continue to start up into his face. The pull to him is intoxicatingly strong. Even faced with the fact he is a Vampire doesn't truly scare me enough to get away from him.

I am truly an idiot....

His grip around my waist is firm with the other arm on my upper back to lock me into place. It looks like I'm not going anywhere any time soon. "So, just like that, you think you can give me an order?" He says smirking down at me. "I'm a vampire and part of the royal court. Not some Patrolman. With that comes great power which includes mind reading." Lucas's smooth voice as he says this is eerie. His cocked eyebrow at the end matched his half-smirk. "So, let's just see what is in that pretty little head of yours shall we?" He leans further in. I feel a slight pressure on the edge of my mind.

Crap, no, I forgot that vampires can do this.

They are very private and usually stay on their side of town.

Ok, I just need to push back to make sure he doesn't see anything. "Aaaaahhhhh!" I say with an edge to my gasp as the pressure increases in my head.

The crease is back between his brows making me want to smooth it out. His fangs lengthen to the point where they cannot be ignored.

Seeing them fully out causes me to squirm in his arms but his hand moves up to the base of my neck to drag me further up his chest. I start to push back with not just my mind but my hands as well. The muscles under my hands flex at the pressure I put into my next push. Still, I am in his hold and getting closer to those fangs. His eyes flash red around the rim showing his other side coming through further.

All of a sudden, the pressure subsides and I can blink away the tears that had welled up from the pressure. I shake my head a little to clear him out the rest of the way. He slowly puts me down but the smirk is gone.

As my feet touched the ground the realization of the fact, I just beat a vampire at his own game was a relief more than a triumph. The crease was still there between his brows with the frown back in place to match. The playful smirk can be just as deadly as his frown I bet. His fangs were still out and his breathing was heavy like he just got done running a marathon.

"What the hell that hurt!....... Get your hands off of me!" I say with a little bit of panic in my voice. I can't stop the shudder as he lets me go and backs away, shaking his head in confusion. "This is not possible. You shouldn't be able to push me out of your head. What are you? How are you doing this?" Lucas calmly asks while leaning on one leg with his arms crossed in front of his chest. He continues to stare at me, not with a glare but with frustration and curiosity.

"Why should I tell you what I am? After the bullshit, you just tried to pull?" I calmly state back to him with an edge in my voice. "As I said before. I am going home where I have a friend to heal me and I will let you know if the vision will help you." While turning towards my car.

I look slightly over my shoulder as he stands by the mucky ash that is almost gone completely. Thinking it might not be a good idea to try to intimidate a vampire but hey I guess that is a little late. Opening my car door, I get a sense that this is not the last time I will be seeing him.

I also missed his arms around me..... Yeah, I hope to have a screw loose.

CHAPTER 3

Well, that was an eventful morning from hell. Pulling onto our street on the Eastside of town I hope that Tori is home and awake. Our part of town was full of misfits like me and my friends.

There are a lot of colorful souls over here.

From your rogue werewolf to fairies and everything in between. It is easy to not have too many people guessing what you are because let's face it, they are probably hiding too.

Our building is five and a half stories tall at the end of the block. With our office on the second floor and then the top two and a half stories are where we live. The building is sandstone with balconies on the floors above. The first floor of the building is two stories because of the balconies that overlook the club on the inside. Our office space was in the bar Apothecary downstairs on the private balcony overlooking the bar.

This comes in handy when it's been a rough night hunting. It is also nice having a backup if a client becomes unhappy. Not only is the owner like a father to us but a lot of our friends work in the bar.

I take the ally on the right side to the back lot that leads to the underground parking for residents. Pulling through the black iron door is like pulling into the belly of a castle. The ruff stone columns supporting the building curve up at the top into ornate art Nouveau ribbing and arms that connect them. The cobblestone floor has seen better days but the patchwork over the years has tried to stay close to what the original stones were.

This place looks like it should have a coach and buggies, not the assortment of cars that are here.

I am glad to see Tori's dark purple mustang parked in the first spot next to where I usually park next to the wall.

We are different when it comes to cars.

I'm more practical and she is all about the flash. I have to hand it to her. When she lets that the engine loose close up. The Mustang can really purr. Chloe on the other hand was all about motorcycles. She had two parked in her usual spot, which I'm sure were much faster than they needed to be.

She likes to find deserted or hardly used roads outside of town. A shiver goes down my spine at the thought of her rolling one of her bikes around a turn.

After I park my car, I make a quick assessment of myself. Yep, definitely filthy and still need Tori to heal me.

Shit, that demon fucked with my morning.

Leaning my head back I curse one more time before slowing down my breathing.

I do a couple more of the slow yoga breaths before I give up.... punching the steering wheel. Crap, that hurt! Why did I have to do that and why did that demon have to show up when I wasn't prepared for a hunt? I just wanted to go for a relaxing, mindless run.

I grabbed my wet pullover from the seat next to me with two fingers. Holding it away from me. Yeah, it smells even worse now than it has been in my car marinating for the last 10 minutes.

Looking back into the car I see that I'm going to have to clean this up right away or this will ruin my seats and that smell could wake even Tori up.

Sighing I start to get my ass moving.

I get out of the car to go over to the workbench and shelves by the back wall. I find the old towels that we use for cleaning down here, they should work. After looking at the pullover on my other hand I just threw it on the ground nearby. Hearing the 'splat' from my pullover made me cringe.

Gross doesn't begin to describe my current state.

I grab the leather cleaner off the other shelf before going to my car. I start by wiping down both seats with one towel and using the second to get the inside of the driver's side door. Then use a third towel to put some leather cleaner on. I hope this works...

Grabbing the mat on the driver's side I grab the hose from the back wall to spray down the mat. I kick off my shoes and spray them too. Saying a prayer for them.

Walking to the shelves again I find some fabric cleaner for cloth seats that I think will work for my shoes. Spraying them, I do another quick assessment of the shoes after the first spray, I spray them again with the fabric cleaner.

I wonder if doing all this even helps. Shrugging, I can't put them in the washing machine like this anyway so might as well try this first, I guess.

My legs are killing me. I need to go find Tori to get this healed. I roll my head back and forth to release some of the tension in my shoulders. While leaning back against Boo.

I know that it isn't the most original name for my black beast but it works.

Giving her one last look over I picked up my shoes and the towels to head to the elevator.

Staggering over to the elevator I breathe a sigh of relief that this thing works. Really hope that it never breaks. I would hate to take all those stairs up. It's one thing to take them down or let's face it jumping off the top of the roof and landing all superhero style is a great pick me up. I pushed the black iron button up.

The black iron gate reminded me of a jail cell every time I used the elevator, I got a chill up my spine. After hearing the ding of the elevator arriving and unlocking the gate. I push the gate aside to climb into the elevator. The panel on the wall has four buttons to choose from. I pushed to number three to get to our two and a half floors thankful that there was no music yet from the club filtering in.

The elevator dinged again when I reached the third floor. I moved the gate aside and walked into our home.

Breathing in the familiar scent of flowers that were around the room. They hung from the ceiling in pots, were on tables, or even spouted from pots on the floor. The first floor is the living room, kitchen, dining, and small water closet under the stairs.

Our taste is most comfortable with a lot of colors. Most of the furniture was found at flea markets. The living room has a large comfy grey couch. We were able to fix the holes and then cover the whole couch with a couch cover that is soft with a velvety grey and white couch cover. There are a lot of colorful pillows with different textures on the couch. With some bigger pillows on the floor leaning against the old fireplace hearth. The tv sat on a stand on the hearth in front of the opening of the fireplace.

We have never used it but right now a fire would feel great. Instead, I turn towards the kitchen to grab some water on the way through the dining room. The cuts on my lower legs and the bruises needed attending.

They are screaming now with every step I take. I wince as I take the next step. I had to pause on the stairs to stop crying out when I tripped hitting the scrapes on the stairs.

"Aahhh.....Crap" I say under my breath.

I walked up the steps to the second floor the rest of the way hoping to find Tori in a good mood. Turning to the closet at the top of the stairs that holds our washer and dryer; I threw the towels and shoes in the washing machine. Which is both liberating and frustrating. What if they don't come clean and even worse if I destroy the washing machine, they will kill me.

Well, I guess I better go wake up Tori. I went to the green door on the right of the upstairs sitting room. Knocking on the door while saying "Tori! I need your help. I got attacked by a demon on the trail. I have some nasty cuts from sliding on the gravel.".......... "Tori! Come on please!" I slowly open her door when saying this last part. Looking for any movement from the lump of blankets in the bed.

She is a cranky person in the morning and not one to mess with.

I walked over to the bed avoiding the mess of clothes from last night when she stripped down to climb in bed. She loved to sleep naked in only her underwear.

The last time I came in here was with Chloe and we had fun trying to land necklaces on her boobs. Kind of like horseshoes. Too bad one of them hit Tori in the face because Chloe got pretty close. Tori had jumped out of bed to chase us out. She forgot that she was naked.

Well, at least this time she was on her stomach with most of her body covered.

Tori opened one eye and gave me the stinky eye with it. She slowly turned over on her side to continue the stink eye. "Ok, ok I'm up, what is wrong? Why are you up so early?" asked Tori.

She finally looked at me and sprang out of bed at seeing me covered in blood and mud. Forgetting that she is naked and grabbing me. "Tori calm down," I say while trying to point to a bathrobe at the end of her bed.

I wonder what would happen if there ever was a fire. Would she come running out of the building naked or would this finally get her to put clothes on?

Shrugging off her hands. "I went to the trail to go for a run because I couldn't sleep. A demon came out of nowhere and started to chase me. I was able to kill it, so no worries." I explained

As she slipped the robe over her tan skin, she pulled her long brownish red hair out of the back of it. Her dark brown eyes just stared at me with an assessing glance.

She is all business now.

Her gaze finally found the cuts on my knees and lower legs. She quickly bent over to look at them. "Let me guess you tripped?" She says with a small laugh. "No, technically I dove out of the way to avoid a lightning bolt, smart ass," I say with a wince as she tries to get a better look at the cuts under my yoga pants. "Hey! Shit, that hurts!" I shout at her.

With all the shouting Chloe comes in with her curly red hair in a mess going down her back. She is wearing a nighty tank and shorts to match. Her hazel eyes are barely open as she walks over to where Tori is bent over still trying to get a better look at my legs. "Ok, what the Hell is going on here. I can hear you at the end of the hallway...... You are a mess, Alex. What happened to you?" Chloe asks with a yawn. She leans against the door from on her right shoulder.

"I will tell you as soon as Tori and her hands from hell back off for a second." Sarcasm comes naturally to me.. Tori responded with. "You wanted my help so stop getting all pissy at me. Now hold still so I can get all the damage in one shot." She slowly moves her hands up and down the injuries with a glow coming from her hands. It only took a few minutes for the cuts to heal up but after they started to itch from the mud and dried blood.

Err yeah need to get this off.

Tori stood up and looked into my eyes while grabbing my shoulders. She said, "Ok you are healed now, explain everything, and don't you dare leave anything out." In the doorway, Chloe just nodded in agreement.

They behaved more like we are sisters than friends but that is ok, we are all we have, after our village was destroyed. To this day we don't know the reason why it was destroyed or why we were the only ones to survive.

I decided to kill two birds with one stone so to speak. "Ok I will explain but I need to get out of these clothes and take a shower. So, follow me if you want or this can wait till I'm done." As I walked past Chloe causing them both to follow me to the bathroom across the hall from Tori's room.

Tori took up residence on the stool by the door and Chloe jumped up onto the counter putting her feet in the sink. She continued to plug the sink and turn the warm water on to soak her feet.

If she is doing this then she went dancing last night in the bar downstairs. She can make anyone drool when she dances. Her curves can entice, not just any man but any woman when she starts to swing those hips.

Tori throws one of the pillows from the bench at Chloe to lean back against the hard stone wall. "Ok is everyone comfy?" I ask with a small smirk on my face. Tori rolled her shoulders while yawning again. Chloe answered for them both by saying "Yep, go ahead."

As they were getting comfy, I had been stripping off the wet clothes and tossed my once favorite purple yoga pants in the garbage with a sigh. The rest of my clothes are salvageable so I throw them on the floor to take to the washing machine. They hit the floor with a splat with Tori and Chloe saying "Gross!"

Well, they weren't wrong. "Yeah, and I had to drive home in them so don't you dare start with me," I say. Tori and her smart mouth retorted. "I give it a couple of days but no promises." Her smile at the end spoke of her sass.

I step into the warm water with another sigh but this one is one of pure bliss. I loved a warm shower; I am naturally on the cold side due to the ice gift that I had gotten after my mother passed it to me at her death. Sure, the cold doesn't bug me like it bugs others but I still like the feeling of the warm water.

The warmth never reached my soul. It was more annoying than anything. But I do have the advantage during winter.

I have never had to buy a winter coat. The weird looks I get during winter are hilarious. I get most of them from regular humans who don't know any better.

A relative can only do this at their death and it has to be willingly given and received for this to happen. Just thinking of her made the longing come back. She was one of the bravest in my life. One of her last acts was to send her magic to me, to better protect myself. I can still hear her telling me she loved me and to run with my friends.

A tear ran down my face before I could stop it. Sniffing back the rest I pull myself back to the present. We all lost people that day. It is best not to bring this up.

"This water feels amazing!" I say while reaching for the shampoo. "Yeah, yeah, yeah start talking or I will get a cup of cold water to throw at you Chica," Tori says with a little bit of her early morning crankiness coming through. I peek out around the shower curtain to see Chloe patiently rubbing her feet in the water and Tori filing her sharp nails.

"Yeah, but you know that it doesn't work on me like it would on Chloe so nice try." I stick my tongue out before ducking back into the shower.

Chloe gives me a knowing smirk with a wink before I get fully back in the shower. She says "Or we are coming in. We have to get ready too, you know." I whip the curtain back into place before continuing with what happened this morning. "Well crap, can't a girl enjoy the water a little bit? Ok, I couldn't sleep this morning. I decided to work on my running on terrain, not pavement. We›re meeting with someone from Kyro Industries tonight for a job. I thought I better get the jitters out." I explained while rubbing shampoo in. I hold in the moan as I massage the soup into my scalp.

"Shit, that's tonight? I thought that it was on Saturday night?" asked Chloe. I could tell she was pouting. "I told Brian I would help out at the bar. A group of high-end clients are coming into the bar tonight and they need extra help." She explained. "Well, I can see if the client can come this afternoon instead." Says Tori picking up her phone. "Yeah, that is fine with me. But you're in charge of texting them since I'm currently naked in the shower." I laughed while washing out the rest of the shampoo.

As Tori texts the clients to see about rescheduling for this afternoon, I continue with what happened this morning. "So, after I got to the trail-head I was just starting to run when a demon came out of the brush. He gave me this weird look with a recognition behind it. He started to run at me so I ran down the path hoping that I wouldn't have to kill him." I say while Chloe jumps in to ask "Why didn't you want to kill the demon? We do that all the time." I respond with "Yes I know but I just wanted a mindless run with my music. I was a little pissed that it wasn't going to happen, so I took off at first. Then he started to throw lightning at me. I tried to avoid it but when I dove to the side I got scraped up a bit."

I could hear the gasps and the "Oh, craps" from in the shower.

Washing the rest of the mud off was the greatest feeling in the world right now.

After rinsing off the mud I continued "After that, I was able to come at him before he was able to get another lightning bolt. I stabbed him in the gut and slashed his throat for good measure.

And yes, before you say anything, I am going to practice my ice gift more. It would have been smarter to not fight him in close quarters." Their faces were in that half-smile and nodding to the last part. Tori spoke up to ask "Did you get the ash and pictures from the demon? We may be able to collect some money for dealing with that kind of demon even though we weren't commissioned."

That would have been a great idea but I am not going to admit that just yet. "Well after I called the Patrol things changed. Not a normal Patrolman showed up. Instead, it was this hot, cocky son of bitch who needed to take it down a few notches." I said getting out of the shower to finish drying off. My mind was racing still but at least I am clean.

"Wait what happened and why is he hot and a son of a bitch?" Chloe said with an even tone with a small smile. Can't even get mad at her for the smile because if anything, getting this all out might help me see why the vision showed up when I touched him. "When he got there, he had this frown already on his face and yes, even that didn't take away from how hot he is," I say because I can see both of them sitting up a little straighter to interject. "The thing is, he didn't get overly bossy till after I had a vision while touching him. The vision included the same demon that I had just killed, but in this vision, I think this one evil guy could see me. I was pulled back before I could confirm this. Kind of glad I did because he and his demons killed four guys before the evil skeleton tattoo guy said to get her!" So, glad I got this last part out.

Walking over to where Chloe still had her feet in the sink with the towel wrapped around me I started to do my morning ritual of face wash and creams.

My cool skin didn't need much but I still believed in self-care.

Chloe pulled her feet out of the water in the sink to drain it. She then grabbed some of my towels to dry her feet while talking to us. "So, you had a vision but usually you see the people of things you touch in them, right?"

But I didn't have an answer for that, but Tori did for me while I was brushing out my long hair. "Yes, whenever you usually have one that happens. Was he in it? What happened exactly?" She asked. "I was definitely in the past judging by the Viking ship and how the four men were dressed. They were loading some crates onto the ship before these demons came down the hill towards the docks. I'm sure they are the same demon species that I killed today at the trail."

"They have Black leathery skin with veins that light up when the lightning is drawn into their bodies. I think that they can summon the lightning because it wasn't raining that hard till they showed up. The lightning was fired at me and those men from their hands. They also have sharp claws and large teeth that they can use for shredding. Those guys didn't have a chance. You should have seen how they died and the looks of sheer shock and horror. It's like they had never seen a demon before." I say facing my friends. Tori was getting up coming towards me and Chloe was still sitting on the counter by me.

Tori just wraps me in a hug while Chloe says "Wow! That's a lot from the past but I agree you were pulled from the vision too soon to see how this connected to this Patrolman and to the demon you just killed." Tori was grabbing me by the shoulders with a concerned look that said I know you aren't done but I hope it doesn't get worse.

Unfortunately, it kind of does.

I look at my two friends and then say "I know you don't want this to get any worse but after I got pulled out of the vision the Patrolman revealed that he is a vampire and not just any vampire. He is in the royal court. His name is Lucas Storm and to get this sense he is a member of the royal court; he can read minds."

"What! Really? I thought that was just a myth?" Tori said while Chloe jumped down to pace in the small room. It was starting to get tight in here. "Good news is I somehow pushed him out of my mind. He said that is not normal and wanted to know what I am." I say to them.

Tori let me go and Chloe opens the door.

She walks to my room with us following behind her. Tori immediately walks to my mini-fridge for a cold coffee and then deposits herself in the cushy teal chair. Chloe goes to my closet and starts throwing clothes at me. "Hey, you know I can pick out my clothes? I'm not a toddler." I say while trying to catch the clothes aimed at my head. "Yes, you can, but I don't think it matters. I have too much to get done now that the meeting is going to be moved up. We need to get to the library to look up this demon before the meeting." Chloe turns while saying, with that don't mess with me look. I look down at the jeans, tank, and leather jacket with a shrug. Walking over to my drawers for my underwear, bra, and socks as Tori's phone goes off.

Tori answered the call "Hi. This is Tori of the Hunters. Yes, I'm sorry about the time change. Would this afternoon work for you?" I wish I could hear the conversation. Tori gives us a thumbs up while talking to the client. "Ok, thanks for understanding. We will see you at one o'clock this afternoon." She gets up from the chair and starts to walk out of the room with Chloe to get ready. I snag the cold coffee out of her hand. "Thanks for opening this for me," I say with a wink as she grabs it back and walks out of the room.

I shut the door to get ready but thought I would need a little luck today, so I went back to my underwear to find a lucky pair. I settled on some seamless booty shorts that have gold pineapples on light pink material. With a light pink bra with a little lace going up the back. I pull on my white socks before pulling on my jeans. The tank is a skin-hugging dark blue with a deep v in front. The deep v has three chains going across the front connecting the two sides. My leather jacket was my signature with my black leather boots with a slight heel. I twist my hair up into a wet messy bun before going out to get something to eat.

Walking past Tori's door is like being at a strip show that has gone through a tornado. She is throwing clothes over her shoulder while only in a thong. "Tori, are you looking for something?" I ask. "Yes, I can't find my favorite jeans with the silver stitching. Have you seen them or did Chloe steal them again?" She responds with an all-knowing look in the direction of Chloe coming out of the bathroom.

Judging by the way she quickly runs to her room she took them.

"I'm not going to rat anyone out or get in the middle of you two again. Last time one of you threw a shoe and hit me, remember." I say with a smirk and laugh at her not so innocent face. She grabs another pair of jeans and a black bra off the chair nearby. "I'm sure if you go in just that little thong the clients will sign right away." Laughing again. "Ha-ha, you know I'm not cheap." She says with a smile and does a hair flip.

I just shake my head turning around to go downstairs. I hear a thump and turn back around to see Tori on the floor with one leg in the pants and the other half in.

Laughing again I turn around to see Chloe fully dressed with her red hair falling down the brown leather jacket over a white tank and tight jeans. "Have you seen my boots? I can't remember if I took them off downstairs or in your room last night." She asks. "Your boots are in my room between the chair and the bed I think," I say remembering her pulling them off before she sat down last night. I walked away to the stairs with Tori finally coming out of her room fully clothed.

I grabbed the coffee from her again and took another swig as we went downstairs. "I'm done with that crap. I need my diesel fuel. That stuff tastes like crap." Tori said. She walked over to the coffee machine that was already pouring out her strong black coffee. I walked over to the fridge for one of the breakfast burritos that we pre-made last weekend. Tori snaps her fingers, so I throw one of the bacon burritos at her.

She catches it and pretends to throw it on the ground. Then she does her touch-down dance. Which looks like a chicken dance mixed with a running man.

God's above I love her even if she is a nerd.

I throw mine and one for Chloe at her, to put in the microwave over the stove. Chloe comes running down the stairs now fully dressed. I grab her a travel mug from the cabinet behind me for her coffee. She goes to the fridge for her caramel creamer before pouring the coffee into the mug. The microwave beeps and Tori grabs the three burritos. "Hot! Hot!" Tori yelped. Throwing two of them back and forth before throwing them to us. She then grabs hers tossing it on the island counter to help cool it off while she takes a drink of her diesel fuel.

Tearing off the top of the wax paper I start to walk to the elevator. The heat feels good in my cold hand. "We need a plan for today," I comment while trying to get a bit of the hot burrito. I burn my tongue but it is worth it.

Chloe pops up "I think we should talk about taking motorcycles, we can park anywhere with them and get to the library faster than one of your cars." This is true. "Yeah, but what kind of tweaking did you do lately? Are they still legal?" I joke.

Tori isn't one to hold back either, she says "Can they still be called motorcycles? I mean with all your tweaks shouldn't we call them beasts or the creation of Frankenstein?" We laugh at our comments while Chloe just gives us the finger. "I like to think of those tweaks as improvements. Thank you very much." She says smugly. She flips some red hair over her shoulder. I love getting under her calm decorum some days.

Smiling to myself I lean up against the back of the elevator smiling at the back of Chloe's head. She had turned to face the doors rather than put up with us. But let's face it she is still trapped for now. Might as well poke at her a little more.

I reach for her hair tugging on it causing her to grunt at me. She turns around with her finger up in the air pointing at me. "Don't you do that again or I will wake you up with a squirt gun next time we need to do some early morning training." Her eyes are full of sass and I know she would follow through with it.

Sighing, I put my hands up in defeat.

The elevator dinged when we reached the lower level. Walking back in here I can't help but glance over at my car.

Chloe continues to make a plan for the day. "After we get to the library one of us should go down the street to ask Freya about the vampire court. Two of us should go into the library to find out about the demon you killed. I think after that we should have time to stop by the bar. Ace and Ellie might be there. Ellie is good with history; she may know more about these Vikings from your vision." She lifts the back seat of her black sleek bike to store our coffee. She built cup holders into the seat as soon as she got them. Because let's face it, who can live without coffee?

If they can, then there is something wrong with them.

We grab the helmets from the shelf in front of the motorcycles. Mine is dark blue, Tori's is black, and Chloe's is Dark purple that fades to black. We all quickly braid our hair or put it in a low ponytail. I opt for braiding my hair which will give my hair even more wave after it dries instead of keeping it in a messy bun. "If we are going to make this a regular thing, we need to get one more bike. I'm so tired of riding bitch." I say. "Well, if you help buy it as Tori did then fine we can get a third bike," Chloe says all smugly and Tori just nods along.

They both back up the bikes then swing their legs over. Chloe waits for me to jump on before starting the bike. I swing up behind Chloe with as much grace as I can manage. I grip her waist while she turns the beast on.

Feeling that rumble between my legs is always thrilling.

Tori opens the garage this time with the button hidden in the compartment on the top of her bike next to the key.

CHAPTER 4

As we approached downtown, the traffic was getting thicker and more aggressive. These people need to chill.

Chloe and Tori whipped around traffic getting honked at by a guy in a Range Rover who I am guessing didn't like when they squeezed by. I laugh and shake my head. We needed to get some microphones or something in these helmets.

We pull up on State Street in front of the library. While cutting the beasts off, the Range Rover guy comes to a stop in the spot behind us.

Crap, this shall be entertaining.

I place the helmet down to grab the two coffees out of the insert. Chloe throws her helmet to Tori. Walking a few steps towards Rover guy.

She cocks her hip and lifts an eyebrow at the guy getting out of the Range Rover. He is pointing his finger at Chloe while yelling. "Are you crazy? You bitch! You could have hit me." Now he is right up in her face. I smile a little while Tori comes over to stand by me for the show.

Chloe takes the guy's hand, yanking the whole arm forward, turning into him, and flips him over her shoulder. Hearing the "umph" that came out of the guy was satisfying. She holds him down with her boot on his throat, leaning in. "Ok, here is the thing. I didn't hit you. You can't intimidate me. You're the one coming at a woman in the street. Who do you think these people are judging? So here is a suggestion: get back into that over-modified thing you call a Range Rover and drive away." She says.

The guy makes a slight nod but judging by the look on his face he will not forget this. Chloe retracts her boot from his throat to take a few steps back. The Rover guy rolls to his side coughing and pushes himself up. The glare he gives us is one of loathing and calculation.

I wave at him and Tori gives him the finger.

I see the vein in the side of his forehead pulse while he clenches his jaw. He makes a grab for Chloe who blocks him then shoots a stream of water at him pinning him to his vehicle.

I hear his head crack back into the hood and the vehicle groans under the impact. But the guy isn't done, his hand shoots out a metal spike. Chloe jumps to the side shooting another jet of water at him. The idiot didn't have the sense to move out of the way. His body for a second time collides with his vehicle. This time he slides down to the ground to slump forward unconscious.

Chloe has perfected her water gift over the years. She can create water that is light as a drizzle to water her plants or strong enough to go through a person. We only know this because of the line of work we are in. A few years ago we were pinned down by a few local gang members that were protecting their boss from being taken in for black-market trading. Tori was knocked out cold and I was being overtaken by 2 of the gang members. She was fighting one with a sword. As she swiped out his feet she had turned, firing a jet of water so powerful it went right through the middle of the guy on my left. Luckily this caused his buddy to hesitate so I was able to hit his knife out of his hand. Taking him down. The rest of the job went pretty well. I think Chloe scared the crap out of them so they only put up half of the fight from the point on.

I pulled my phone out of the inner pocket of my jacket to call for a second time today the Patrol.

This is one shitty morning.

A woman steps out of the crowd, she looks to be some kind of bird shifter. Judging by the sharp features and graceful movements I would bet on this. She comes over to where we are standing and says. "I called the Patrol after your friend had him pinned to the ground with her fancy boot. They will be here any minute. I also asked my niece to film it with her phone." As she is saying all this a black sleek car pulls up with Patrol plates. The lights in the back window of the car are flashing and the way that the car is parked we weren't going anywhere soon.

I reached over squeezing Tori's hand who had turned her back on them to hide her face. Seeing one of the Patrolmen where I could see why.

Miles came around the hood of the car and his partner went to tell the other Patrol vehicle what to do. Miles is a cheating bastard who thinks that what he did wasn't cheating because he is a guy.

Yep, full douchebag, can't believe to this day that she even dated him for a couple of months before finding out that he was also dating two other girls but Tori should be fine with it, and mind you, they had agreed to exclusively dating each other. He then went on to explain that it was ok because men have needs that not just one woman can satisfy. That even when he gets married this will continue because women know, men need more than any one of them can provide.

Thank the Gods there were people at the next table or I think she would have killed him.

I wish I had been there when this had all gone down. I still to this day feel like he deserves a punch to the face or a knee to the groin.....maybe both depending on if it would help him see that he is an idiot.

Miles came over to us but stopped mid-stride when he realized who he was approaching. He hung his head saying "Shit! Rick, get over here. Ask these ladies to give their statements." He walked over to the unconscious Rover Guy. Bending over he smacked him in the face to wake him up. That didn't work so he walked back over to the car. I saw him grab the first aid kit out of the trunk then slowly walk back. He took something small out of the kit and placed it under the guy's nose. Judging by the guy waking up it is Smelling Salts. So glad this is when the swan shifter lady spoke up. "Hi, I'm Rose Carlson. I'm the one who called you and my niece filmed it with her phone." She motioned for her niece to come closer.

Rose handed the phone to Rick. Rick watched the whole thing before speaking up. "OK thank you, ma'am. This was very helpful if you could please stick around. I will need to get that video and your statement. Please stand on the curb with your niece." After that, he looked over at us before taking a visibly deep breath and exhaling before walking over to us,

Tori turned around with fire in her eyes looking in the direction of Miles then focusing on Rick. Cloe decided to start. "I think you know who we are, judging by who your partner is. But just in case I'm Chloe. This is Alex". Pointing to me. "And this is Tori." She placed her hand on

Tori. Rick gave her a stern look. "Yes, I do recognize your friend Tori more but yes, I remember you and Alex as well. Judging by that video on that woman's phone you were defending yourself from the gentleman on the ground over there. All I need from you ladies is your statements then we will be taking this guy in." He motioned for a few more of the officers to come over telling them to take our statements and get a tow truck down here for the Range Rover.

Seeing them get that guy off the ground and into the back of the Patrol car was satisfying and I let out a breath I didn't know I was holding in. After that seeing Miles ducking his head and glaring at Tori just put my back right up again.

Why the hell would he be glaring at her? She wasn't the one cheating. I turn to give Tori a look that says *what gives*, but she just shook her head while going to give her statement to one of the other officers. Fine by me but this is not over.

After we all give our statements, I go over to Tori and pinch her in the side causing her to say "Hey! What was that for?" I give her a side glance with an eyebrow lift saying. "You know perfectly well what that was for and believe me, you will be spilling those guts later with all the juicy details." She just rolled her eyes and started to get up on the curb to walk to the charms store to talk to Freya.

Yeah, she can run right now, later I'll just get her drunk for the whole story.

I saw Miles give her one last glare before he pulled away for the tow truck. At this point, the Rover guy is yelling at Miles and Rick that it was not his fault. Rick just turned around opening up the slider for the barrier glass and punched him in the face causing the guy to pass out again.

I shake my head while muttering "Some people's kids." Causing Chloe to throw her head back laughing. I linked our arms together pulling her in close, resting my head on hers for a second. "If you are going to keep having these fights let me know ahead of time so I can collect bets from the bystanders," I ask with a smirk. "Sure will! And you had better double down because you know I don't lose," she said brightly with a wink.

Going into the library was like a religious experience. Taking that first inhale of the books just fed my soul. The smell of all those pages just adds to the atmosphere of adventure. For every book contained, one is just waiting for the right person. Even the books that are for research had a story to tell, though some were more important.

Walking up to the receptionist I handed over my ID for her to scan. My Hunters' license gives me access to the back part of the library. Where all the books about demons, forbidden magic books, and history of some-things left to forget for that history is too powerful to be repeated.

The receptionist eyed me but gave me back my ID and took Chloe's next. After that the receptionist said, "Ok, everything seems to be in order. Take all the time you need. I presume you know where you are going?" I smiled at her because she knew. We come here quite a bit for information on the demons and bad guys that we hunt. "Yep, we know the way." As I hold out my hand and also say. "I'm Alex and this is Chloe. We come here a lot. It's nice to see a new face." She looks shocked at the hand that is thrust in front of her. She slowly takes the tips of my fingers, shakes it once, and says. "Umm yes, I just started a few days ago. My name is Qwen." She immediately casts her eyes back down and shifts to the other side of the desk to look at the computer.

Ok, so that was strange. I look at Chloe who just shrugs her shoulders tilting her head to the right. Motioning for us to head to the back of the library. Passing the bookshelves, I see a couple of ghosts sitting up on the top.

They look to be arguing about a book that another is waving around overhead.

Chloe pulls me along knowing that I can't resist a good book discussion. Sometimes it sucks when a person knows you so well. I shake my head at her with a frown saying. "Spoil! Sport!" She laughs and shushes me. "Yes, I am! Now be good or no ice cream for you," she says sarcastically.

I just hang my head laughing like an idiot.

Reaching the old mahogany doors with beautiful flowers carved into the border of the door and a tree on both doors in the middle. I prick my finger to give the door a little blood for entry. Chloe does the same on the other door. The wood soaks up the blood. Then pulses slightly and opens.

I can see someone duck behind the bookshelf nearby. I hold up my hand for Chloe to wait a second. Walking over to the shelf and peering around the corner I see nothing.

Weird, I could>ve sworn there was someone there.

"What? Is someone there?" Chloe asks with a pitch to her voice. She is definitely on alert if her voice gets higher. I shrug and shake my head. "I guess not but I would have bet that someone just ducked behind here. Looked a little like the woman at the front desk. I still have that feeling of someone watching us."

We both take one last look around ourselves before entering the back part of the library.

The door shuts heavily behind us.

Every time I don't know why but I jump. We come here all the time and it always shuts like a ton of bricks.

Chloe wanders over to the demon section. While I go over the history of magic to see if there is anything about Vikings or a guy with a skeleton tattoo. This could take us a couple of hours but thankfully they let you take some of these book's home.

After about forty minutes I heard. "Hells yeah! I think I found your demon." Chloe shouts across the room. I'm sure she is doing some form of a touchdown dance.

I jump up from the floor running across the room down some isles.

She holds up her hand for a high five then as we both come down we smack each other's asses. "Hahaha" I laugh at us, for if guys can slap each other's asses for a good job why can't we.

She hands me the book that looks to be a couple of decades old. The black leather binding is ruff and the pages have yellowed. Thankfully the ghosts take the time to oil a few books every day or these books would be in really bad shape. I can't even think about all that could be lost if they didn't do this.

Sitting down on the ground, propped up against the bookcase. I set the book across my thighs to see the demon from earlier staring back up at me.

The muscular black leathery body with glowing veins. The demon's mouth was pulled back to reveal those jagged teeth under a blunt nose and greyish white eye. Black hair spilled down the back of the demon.

Seeing the demon again sent chills up my spine which is a feat since I can manipulate ice.

I finally look at the name below the hand-drawn picture. "Fulmine Nero," I say out loud. Looking at Chloe I can see she has already read it. Her Gaze is intensely on me waiting for me to finish reading. I continue to read now to myself.

Fulmine Nero's are a lower demon. These demons are one of the easier ones to get out of hell. They are usually used in armies due to them fighting better in numbers. When alone the demon may have muscle and some speed but any supernatural with some training should be able to kill it. They are not the smartest creatures and need a lot of direction from those that let them out.

The Lightning that the demon creates to absorb will hurt but not kill a person on the first hit. Though it will wound a person. They are also known to carry some kind of sword or knife.

Fulmine Nero has black leathery skin over large muscles on a tall frame. The skin will have veins running close to the surface that will be visible, especially when the lightning is absorbed and then fired at their intended target. The face is going to be wide set with a blunt nose to match. The mouth has jagged sharp teeth that can cut through bone. The eyes have a haunted look. They are greyish white with some light in them. Mainly this light is what is left over from what they absorb from the lightning.

If one comes across a Fulmine Nero kill on site. They can not be trusted without a master.

Leaning my head back against the shelf I looked over at Chloe who had started to look through another book. Her phone beeps as I start to get up from the floor.

Next time we should bring the books over to the fireplace. Those couches and chairs are way better than the floor.

I took a couple of pictures of the page from the book to show Tori. I hate trying to relay info when I can just shove it at a person instead. Chloe had put the other book down to answer the message I am assuming is from Tori. "Tori got some useful information from Freya. She also stocked up on some poisons and charms. Freya will be coming to the bar later; she wants a drink for her info and to hang out." Chloe relayed from her phone. I laugh knowing our friend could always be trusted, not just for information but having our backs.

"I was looking at some of the books in the history section and what I read about the Vikings is that they were like their normal humans and some supernatural brethren. They stole and pillaged, taking what they wanted, including an occasional person. Other than that, they lived in villages close to the shore. A lot of their lives revolved around the sea. The trade between villages wasn't as violent as when they were pillaged by another nationality. I didn't get a good look at what they were putting on the ship but I didn't see any so-called prisoners." I try to explain this to Chloe as we are walking back to the regular section of the library.

"The supernatural's were called Berserkir or Berserkers. They say that those who have powers are blessed by Odin himself. That may be why they weren't surprised by the demons that attacked them with the man." I turn to Chloe pulling up short at the door. "I wonder if they had any gifts?" Chloe murmured

The doors open by themselves to let us through and just as we step through again I see Tori coming towards us. She has two books under her arm and a bag hanging from her other hand.

She hands me the bag of items from Freya's shop. "I accidentally also found some books that needed to come home with me." she smiled with a wink.

I roll my eyes at the bad joke reaching out to look at the covers of what she found. Seeing the bloody scene on the cover confirmed that my friend was going to have nightmares. She always went for the blood and gore.

Whenever she reads one of these books, I hear a tap on my door and then feel her crawling into bed with me from her overactive imagination getting ideas from these books.

I shake my head at her and point a finger and say "If you get those books you have to be a big girl and sleep in your 'OWN' bed. Last time you pushed me out of bed with your foot, to be in the middle of the bed. If you can't learn to share my bed, then you are out of luck." Flicking her nose as she just smiles knowing I would never turn her away.

Chloe laughed at us and decided to add. "I'm with her. Last time you came to my bed, with not a stitch of clothing on. I didn't realize until morning, you idiot. Talk about boundaries crossed." Tori's cheeks glowed, turning pink for a split sec.

Well, Chloe wasn't affected by this one bit. "I guess getting your naked ass smacked at six in the morning is a good reminder." She said smacking her ass as she walked next to Tori.

Causing her to yelp and a few people to shush her.

As we neared the front, I waved them off saying "I'll meet you guys out front. I have to make a call." Shifting the bag so I could get to my phone.

I scroll down till I get to Brian's number. Hitting call, I wait leaning against the entrance of the library. It relays me to his voicemail. "Hey, Brian can you have a spot for Freya saved up at the bar? She wants to come by for a drink and you know how she hates having to get her spot." After leaving this message I realized that we had to get a move on to make this meeting. Chloe raided the seat to put the bag into the back compartment.

Next time, I will remember a backpack, that bag barely fits.

The ride back home was just as fast and with just as many horns blaring as we passed them. I just held on and enjoyed the ride ignoring them.

My mind did trail back to the hot vampire. The feeling of missing his touch was still there. I have never felt this before. I will have to look this up on my own.

CHAPTER 5

Getting off the elevator, I walk over to the fridge to pull out the cold coffee. Tori joins me but takes another breakfast burrito out. Throwing another one at Chloe as she is going upstairs to change.

Her clothes got a little scuffed up from the rover guy.

She snags it before it hits the wall yelling "Thanks, I'll be back." Sighing I take one also out for myself. We needed to get some more food in this place. Sighing, I take one last look into our sad fridge.

I ate the burrito lounging in my spot on the couch kicking my boots off.

Running all the detail by Tori as we ate and waited for Chloe to get her ass down here. I hand her the phone so she can look at the description of the demon. That demon freaked me out a bit. I don't have enough information from the vision to understand why I had it.

I'm still surprised at how the vision came to be. Touching Lucas must have triggered it. The demon didn't trigger it. I touched him several times going through his pockets and nothing happened. I still have no idea why he was wearing that necklace.

Not many demons wore jewelry.

Lucas is somehow connected to this. Leaning my head back, shutting my eyes I can see in my mind's eye the piercing blue eyes with the smirk showing some of his extended canine teeth. The feel of his breath on my face was like a caress of his hand. He is so close I could close the gap to meet those lips, feel the fangs graze my lip, and down my neck would be pure heaven. I moaned, catching Tori's attention. "Hey, that sounds like a good or frustrating daydream. Which is it and am I in it?" She jokingly says.

I fling a tomato at her feeling my cheeks turn red. I shift on the couch to face her chair trying to shake off the daydream. "Well, since I know you so well it is not about you," I say with a little sass. "Ok getting back to the demon. I think that is the one from my vision and if you look at the picture on my phone it›s a ninety percent match. We also found a little on the Vikings of the time, but they are pretty normal. They pillage, steal, sail, and live just like humans. If they had gifts then they were called Berserkir or Berserkers.

They didn't even get a chance to use their gifts, even if they had them. They grabbed swords first so it can go either way." I will try to explain. Taking a drink of coffee, instead of alcohol because it is too early for my signature mojito.

But let's face it if we didn't have clients coming soon today would be a great day for day drinking. Making me think about that country music song Day Drinking by Little Big Town.

Humming this song, I take a drink of the coffee and smile over at Tori as she starts singing the lyrics. She stands up to start swinging her hips, using what's left of her burrito as a microphone.

Laughing, I see Chloe coming down shaking her head but she joins in with the dancing. Seeing those two bumping hips singing into their burritos I jump up onto the old coffee table. Putting one of my arms up with my legs spread apart to brace myself I then jump off doing a rocker kick in the air before landing in my superhero pose with one knee bent and a fist into the ground. Standing up the girls are now laughing the last of the lyrics out. I continue to hum it as they finish. "Why don't we do a little day drinking?" they belt out.

We collapse into the chairs and couch with an umph before getting more serious. I shift to pick up my coffee off the table before one of the girls can snag it. Leaning back, I say. "Now that the concert is over, what did you find when you went to see Freya?"

Tori had a mouth full of burrito so I decided to also ask her about Miles on top of this. "You also need to explain why your ex was not just shooting daggers but avoiding you like the plague. You're welcome to answer either question first." I place my hands folded under my head to wait but judging by the glare she is giving me I would pay for my intrusion into her personal life.

I frankly didn't care. She pulled this crap on me all the time.

Chloe just laughed. "Ok let's focus on what Freya said. We can always get into her shit later. We have a client coming in forty-five minutes."

"Sorry. You're right, we can discuss personal business over a cocktail later," I say, cheering her with my cold coffee. She just rolls her eyes with an "argh".

After she sits up she continues. "Freya said that she has heard of Lucas and he is in the Vampire Court but he is not just in it. He is becoming the next king. Don't you remember a couple of weeks ago there was a fight that broke out downtown at that fancy restaurant Sky? Well king Darius was killed during it along with a few of the other high-ranking members of the court. She says that the ones who did this got away. They also had some demons that attacked them recently before this during a trip to Seattle Washington. She didn't know what they looked like but judging by the fact Lucas showed up after you killing a demon may point toward the Fulmine Nero demon. I bet he never reported the demon to the Patrol office either."

Chloe leaned forward rubbing her temples. "If this is true, then we are now on their radar. Shit! We are going to have to be careful about how we go forward with this. They don't like interference from other species. We are descendants of Valkyries but we can't let them know this. You know we are rare and others want to collect us for their gain." She says sternly.

This we have to drive into our heads every day.

For we are rare and powerful.

The only thing is we are young and don't have our gifts at full power yet. As we reach 25 the rest of our abilities come to the surface so to speak.

I will be turning 25 next month on April 22nd. We plan on having a private party because we have no idea what will happen or what will be shown to those present at the time when I was born.

I can hear the clock ticking closer to this time of 9:40 am. I shiver thinking about what is to come. The only thing is that I am glad I'm going first. This way, they will be prepared when they hit their birthdays.

"Ok, the thing is the vision only came forward when I touched him. I may have to see him again to get the rest of the vision. This skeleton tattoo guy I think could see me in the vision. This may be a sign of my powers coming to the surface due to my birthday." I say pulling on my boots.

As we get closer to our 25th birthday we were to develop into full maturity. I believe this happened so the mind and body weren't overwhelmed. Giving us a chance to harness our full potential.

I didn't want to know what happened if we didn't. Shaking off the feeling of the unknown I get up motioning to them to do the same.

It's time to go downstairs to the office so to speak. They take my queue and get up, walking to the door under the stairs that lead down to the balcony area. "Yes, it could be that your powers are coming to the surface at a gradual pass instead of all at once as we thought. Was there anything else that you noticed that seemed off?" Chloe asked, opening the door, stepping through to walk down.

Tori turns on the first step to look at me waiting for me to answer. "Yeah, my wings also came out. I didn't think anything of it but now that I am, they did feel different. Like stronger, I could feel a current of energy zip through them before I was able to pull them back in." I am trying to explain but it is hard. I don't use my wings that often.

The shock towards the end of the realization makes me feel scared. Tori reaches forward, giving me a reassuring squeeze on my hand.

I give her a small smile to reassure her.

We continue to walk down the stairs. I take a deep breath, "We will have to come up with something. Between the demon, vampire, and my vision we need more information. Let's win this client over first then rally later." Saying this at the base of the stairs before walking out of the purple-black door. They agree to this as we walk around the corner to our balcony office.

I pull the heavy curtain to the side walking over to the wall in the corner. I found the spot by the corner above the baseboard. Pushing this. The door to our files opens.

I grab the one for Kyro Industries. Tossing it over to Chloe. Knowing she would talk first.

She has a little more of that innocent look until you piss her off. People tend to relax when she starts talking.

I walk over to the balcony's edge. Looking down, seeing the bar area set up for tonight. Ace was behind the bar helping set up. Carrying the keg over to the hookups with all the muscles showing from his black tight tank. I wave the girls over pointing down at Ace.

Tori starts with the catcalls and we follow. "Hey, muscles, you come here often. I could surely use a strong man's help." I call down, causing the wait staff to snicker.

Brian walks out giving us a smirk before saying "This man is not for sale ladies!" I reply with a "Too bad, would have made you a fair offer." Laughing at Ace's red face, I jumped down landing easily. Chloe and Tori follow my move.

"Sorry Ace, you make it so easy." Winking at him. He turns around saying "I may be easy but only for Ellie" He waves Ellie over as she comes into the bar.

Her bouncing blonde curls are pulled back into a messy bun showing off her delicate European bone structure. Her eyes lock on Ace like he is a beacon. Her full plush lip's part into a smile. She waves back walking over to the bar.

Her little frame of 5"2" doesn't stop her from jumping up onto the bar swinging her legs over to pulling Ace into her for a very steamy kiss.

They were great together.

His steady disposition to her spunkineity was just the right combination. Then seeing his beautiful mocha skin next to her alabaster was like seeing the cream being poured into some rich dark coffee.

They finally part after Tori clears her throat loudly saying "Ok ok, you're definitely off the market." They laugh pulling apart. "Yep, and don't you know I'm the one you negotiate with. Oh! And there is a black SUV pulling onto the street. Don't you guys have clients coming in later or are they early?" she asks.

Chloe waves holding up the file saying "Yep we moved the meeting up so we could help out with the big shots that are coming in. I'll go see if it's them. You guys better go upstairs. Brian, could you have a pitcher of water sent up with some glasses? If they want anything besides that we will bring down the order."

We all follow her lead.

Brian just grunts at her as he lifts the keg in place.

Ace pulls Ellie fully behind the bar, setting her near the limes and lemons that I'm guessing is his hint to start cutting. I turned to walk back up but then remembered I wanted to ask her about the Viking's history.

I walk back up to the bar to ask. "Ellie, can we meet up later? I have some questions about the Vikings." She tilts her head to the side causing some of her curls to fall out of her messy bun. Giving me that squint with a wrinkled nose. She knows something is up but won't pry in front of other people, thank the Gods.

After a pause, she answers. "Yeah, that should be fine. Can we meet tomorrow morning for coffee? I'm working till close and have a paper due tomorrow morning." I just shrug saying "Yeah, that should be fine. Text me after you get done handing it in. I can't believe you>re waiting until the last minute again."

Knowing last time, she vowed to never do that again.

She laughs when Ace says "Don't go there. I have been on her tail about this all week.." She shoots out her tongue at him saying "You know I do my best work under pressure."

At this point, I knew I was only going to get in the way. "Ok, yep not getting in this. I'll see you tomorrow." Hurrying away up the stairs to the balcony.

Looking over my shoulder I can see the playful butt smack Ellie gives Ace. They are way too cute even for a romantic like me. I hope they never realize that they are the cheesy romantic scenes from a movie.

If I didn't love them so much, I would either be sick all the time or have to kill them.

Not many people have that kind of love.

Reaching the balcony I do a quick scan of the space seeing that everything was in its place. Tori waved her hand causing the curtain to shut; drowning out the noise from below.

My powers were almost to that point but until then, I said the words. Sitting down at the so-called head of the table by Tori she leans over. "You may not want to touch anyone else today. We can do some tests later after this before tonight but we really should see what is going on first with your gift." She is right but crap. "Shit you're right, but how the hell am I supposed to not do that with these clients. If I don't shake their hands then they might think something is wrong and well it's rude." I finish saying. I could see the wheels turning in her head. I hear Chloe coming with the clients talking to them softly.

Tori points to the corner behind us by the curtain saying. "Ok, you're right but sit over there... on the ledge of the balcony. Look like you're standing watch by holding the curtain a little open. Do a wave, with one of those head nods to them for the greeting. I promise after this we will go upstairs and do some tests." She is a genius.

Bouncing up I walk over getting up on the ledge in time for Chloe to walk in with the clients from Kyro Industries. I peer out looking down to give them the feel of what I am doing way over here on my own.

Let's face it the person sitting in a dark corner is always preserved as the weirdo, don't trust that person.

As Tori goes around to shake their hands Chloe lifts her eyebrows and bobs her head to the left to show her confusion. Thankfully Tori comes to my rescue. "Hi, I'm Tori. We talked earlier. Thanks for changing the time of our meeting today. Alex will be watching below for anything that could interfere with our meeting today." She gestured to me.

This is my que, I guess.

I incline my head into a bow doing a small wave with my index finger. Shifting myself again gives the impression that I am there to do security.

The four men and two women inclined their heads back with the man closest to Chloe clearly as the leader. "If you believe there to be a problem then I would prefer one of mine to be at the bottom of the stairs and one to be over by your associate." He said this as more of a statement than a question.

I shrug at my friends for they look to me to handle this one. I guess I am the one in charge of security today.

This was getting weird. I hate going off-book.

I can't think of a way to refute this. "That is fine if this will make you feel more comfortable."

He waves his hand towards two of the men at the back without even looking. This man is used to giving orders. But with him bringing his hand up I realize he is wearing gloves. Looking at all the hands that I could see were gloved. This is unusual in more ways than one right. I don't know of anyone who wears gloves indoors, especially leather gloves.

On the men, they remind me of driving gloves and on the women, they look like the gloves that ladies used to wear in the 1700s or 1800s. I know I am more aware of hands due to the tattoo I saw on the men in my vision but crap they could even be coming back into style or they could be germaphobes.

Ok, I should probably say something or at least stop staring. I mentally slap myself out of my crazy thoughts. I need to stay focused on this to be a success.

One of his, I guess bodyguards, is coming over to stand by me. He is thickly built like a bull with a face only a mother could love. He has short military-cut brown hair that emphasizes his thick skull that I'm sure would hurt to punch.

I think I would still try but maybe start with a bob to the right with a punch to the gut to get him to bend over closer to me. Then do a round kick to the side of his face to bring him down.

My legs were the powerhouse to my fight club skills.

I inclined my head at him once again. He did the same, taking me up by the wall behind me. Yeah, this made me very uncomfortable. Turning to him, I motion with my head and eyes to move to the other side. He smirks but does move to the other corner of the curtain.

Chloe starts the meeting off; thank the Gods she didn't even bat an eye at all the changes. "Ok, now that we are situated and comfortable, I think it is time to start. In a few moments, a member of the wait staff will be bringing water but if there is anything else you would like the kitchen is open at this time. There are menus for you to look at if you so choose." She says offering a menu to them. The lead guy shakes his head no, saying "That will not be necessary. I would like to continue with this as quickly as possible. Please."

A staff member named Carl came in quietly. He placed the water pitcher and glasses on the table. "Will there be anything else?" He says to Chloe. "No thanks for bringing us the water." She replies. He nods before exiting. I like it when they come in before a meeting is too far along.

After He left Chloe went on. "Ok, Mr. Loriek, you asked for a meeting but didn't specify who or what we are hunting down for you. I think at this point you should take it from here. I will inform you that we did our research and I know for a fact that your company may be well known but as of a couple of months ago it is in the red. We do not work for free. Therefore, how do you intend to pay us if your company is in the red?" The two women looked taken back on this. The other man beside Mr. Loriek stood up with both hands on the table trying to look threatening I suppose.

His greased back hair that was too long for this did a small jump with him. I tried not to laugh but I had to look out of the curtain to hide the fact I am biting my lower lip in doing so. He then said, "This is not possible, how did you get a hold of our account information? We demand that you keep this to yourself and that you tell us who has given this information to you."

Tori stood up slowly like a cat getting ready to play with her prey. She put one hand on the table leaning into it to give some back to the greased haired monkey.

"We do our research about any potential client. For we don't want to be on the wrong side of this if this all goes down the rabbit hole. Instead of trying to intimidate us, take it for what it is. We're ensuring our safety and payment in this transaction. So please sit back down or we will call this meeting over with. Trust me you don't want anyone else; we are good at what we do. Also, your fly is down" she says with a nod to his open pants. Oh God, this is too much! I turn my head to the curtain once again hiding my laugh.

After the man frantically turned around, pulling up his fly, he sat back down. The glare that he gave Tori is one of pure rage. I wanted to go across the room and kick his high-end ass.

But alas, I couldn't move if I did, I am pretty sure that bodyguard would attack. Mr. Loriek put his hand on the greasy-haired man's arm and harshly told him to calm down.

I think I had better interrupt this thing before it gets out of hand. "As Tori said we do our homework so to speak. Mr. Loriek I'm sure you did the same with us." I'm sure he didn't find much besides our previous hunts; everything else about us is strictly for us. "Could you please continue with what you are here for?" I say calmly, still lounging on the ledge.

His head nodded in my direction before continuing. "Alright, but please keep this information to yourself. We had an issue with person-nel stealing from the bank accounts and the experimental department. I require you to track down the experiment they took and also bring the ones responsible back to me, to deal with. The authorities do not know about what has happened and we would like to keep it that way, to ensure the company's good name."

His dark brown eyebrows form a straight line as he sternly looks across the table. He then hands over a folder that one of the women slid over to him. "Here is the information that you will need to do this. The two employees who stole from us used fake names but there are a few pictures of them. As for the experiment here is a description but do not touch it, break the container, or use it. The name of the experiment is A-344. It is in a clear vial and it will appear blue" After this, he motioned to the file that we were given.

Chloe leaned towards Tori for them to look it over. I stayed right where I am. I trust what they decide. Besides, the grease monkey was eyeing us up like he wanted to start a fight. The woman closest to him placed a hand on his arm with some pressure saying very quietly "Behave." She then nodded in my direction.

I found this funny as I had taken out my dagger to play with. Tossing it up in the air to then catch it without looking at it is a great trick and usually, people were smart not to start anything.

Still playing with my dagger I looked down to see that the staff had set up everything and were filing into the kitchen for the day>s breakdown.

Well, at least they would be out of the way if this got nasty. Looking at the big guy in the other corner seeing him with his hand inside of the suit. I get the feeling that if we don't take this job they wouldn't kindly walk away.

I think that it is time for me to be more than the weirdo in the corner.

Jumping off the ledge freaked out the bodyguard guy. He pointed his gun in a flash at me saying "Don't move any further.>> Well, this guy is in for a rude awakening when it comes to threatening me.

Laughing a little I catch my knife, sheathing it on my holster on my leg." Calm down, big guy. I'm only getting up to tell your boss that we accept. The only stipulation is that it will be doubling the regular price. For you are asking more than originally disclaimed to us." I say. Lifting an eyebrow in Mr. Lariek's direction waiting for him to calm his guy down. Mr. Lariek waves his hand at the bodyguard. "Yes, you are correct that there is more that is required. I will pay you the extra for this. I also think it would be a good idea to have two of my men come with you to help secure the ones who stole from me." said Mr. Loriek.

The bodyguard walked over to stand behind his boss which means he would be one of those men. Well, that can't happen. We didn't need his help with our job and I don't like a trigger-happy idiot on my team.

"Thanks for the offer but we work better with just the three of us. We will get in contact with you after we have the experiment and those that stole from you." I say walking up behind my friend's chairs. Getting a little more weirded out on the situation.

Clients never give us back up. Something is off. Mr. Loriek gets up with his people following. After his people are standing behind him he says. "I strongly suggest you take my men. The people you are going after are dangerous." Chloe stood up with Tori moving around the table. I followed but decided to play with my dagger again.

Leaning my hip on the table to seem more relaxed I start to play my game of catch.

Chloe calmly steps up to him with Tori off to her left. Seeing this I had a pretty good guess on what she wanted me to do with that knife. I look at the others behind Mr. Loriek, who are very tense compared to their boss. I took a quick assessment of what gifts I could feel in the room. Two with fire and one was a shifter. The bodyguard was the shifter guessing some kind of ox or bull. The last one has a metallic aura about him so I'm thinking something to do with metal.

As I didn't do anything dangerous last time with the dagger, they didn't even get their guards up. Underestimating people is always bad, even when you are in a public place like this bar.

Chloe gets about a foot in a half away from the boss before she says. "We thank you for your concern but like Alex said we are good on our own." She holds up her hand, snapping her fingers once just as the dagger reaches my hand. I throw the dagger at her hand. She grabs it out of the air without looking, holding it up to Mr. Lorieks neck. "We know what we are doing. We are Hunters and are highly trained. I believe our meeting is over. If you want us for the job Tori will be handing your man to the left an account to deposit three-fourths of our payment by tonight at midnight. Then we will call you when the job is done." She backs up throwing the knife back over her shoulder at me.

I catch it putting it away.

I continue to lean on the table. I nod at Tori who gives the account card to the grease monkey who has a fireball in his other hand ready to use. Mr. Loriek glares once before adjusting his tie. "I will leave and discuss this further with my colleagues but never threaten me like that again. For you will not like the outcome for yourself if anything is to happen to me." He says stepping back with a set scowl in place with a more than necessary high and mighty tone.

Tori pipes up to say. "This may be true, but you should also remember we don't take any crap from anyone. So don't threaten us. We look forward to the job." She holds out her hand to indicate that this is the end of the meeting. Chloe does the same but I just continue to lean on the table bowing my head to the side as my goodbye.

I turn back around as Tori flicks her wrist moving the curtains back. Walking up to the ledge I peer down watching them leave. As the last one goes through the door, I turn around to find both Chloe and Tori engrossed in the file in front of them. "That was one of the weirdest meetings we have ever had and that includes the one with that slime thrower. I think we better bring this upstairs and talk about this some more. Something seems off." I say moving around the table to go to our door in the hallway.

CHAPTER 6

Sitting around the kitchen island we start to go over the information. There isn't enough there to give us a sense of if this client is going to be a good one to help. Why did these employees take the experiment? What is the experiment? What does it do? Why are they not going to the authorities? These questions I know are not just in my head.

I turn to Tori looking at her scowl while studying the file. "Ok this is crap; we are all thinking it. Whatever this thing is, I don't think it is legal. These people who took it are either the bad guys or the good guys. The fact is Mr. Loriek didn't seem innocent. Even his aura seemed off. I know you felt it?" Asking Tori. Her being a healer gives her the ability to read people a little more closely to their core.

This not only helps when she is healing someone but what is going on in their bodies as well which means the gifts that are running through them. A person can hide some from her but she is pretty powerful. "Well reading his subordinates wasn't that hard. They were all tainted. They practice some darker arts but to see what kind or how they practice I would need to tap into each soul. Mr. Loriek is the hardest to read. His aura is red with a black tint to it and his soul is tainted more than the others." She says, her face is showing her frustration and she is holding her temples like she is getting a headache.

Chloe reaches over and gives her a side hug around the shoulders saying. "Look, don>t sweat it. We will put this away for now." Tori leans in for support. "I think that is a good idea for now. I should go up to the roof for some practice on my ice gift and you guys should practice too. I think with all the changes we will need to be in top form."

Walking up to the stairs, to the right of Chloe's door we can access the metal spiral stairs that lead up to the roof. The lush greenhouse takes up half the rooftop as the last level of the building. I loved walking through Chloe's plants. Feeling them around me was like getting a hug from Chloe. Everything here came from her soul. Chloe stopped to check on her plants, so Tori and I continued to the other side to go out onto the roof.

Looking over my shoulder at Tori I ask. "What kind of test do you think we should do?" I wait as she looks around outside at the various practice setups. Her face brightens and she points over to the targets. "Let's start with your ice gift."

Nodding my head, I step out quickly and walk over to the targets by the chimney to recenter it. Walking back a few steps I raise my hand. Feeling the cold running through my veins. Tunneling that cold through my veins towards my outstretched hand. I drop the temperature at the surface of my skin to make the ice stronger to pierce the round target ahead. Bracing myself I let the ice out.

Shit! It came out way too fast and way too big.

The ice spear that I created shot through the air to the chimney. In my defense, it hit the target. The chimney exploded from the impact at the base of it. Tori came running overtaking me to the ground for cover. And Chloe ran out of the greenhouse.

I don't think my gift has ever been able to do that before. Looking at the destroyed chimney over Tori's shoulder, this was an *oh shit, I am in trouble* moment. "What the hell happened?!" Chloe yelled. "Are you ok?" Tori asked me.

After getting up I said, "Yeah, I'm ok. I think I may have overdone it. I didn't know I could do something that big or destructive. I have never created a spear that large or with the velocity before today." Looking down I still had some ice on that palm of my hand. Brushing it off on the back of my pants I walk over to our poor chimney. "I know a spell that will put this back to rights. *Ridare ai diritti*!" Chloe said, directing her hand at the broken pieces of the chimney. A low green light emanated from her hand. The broken brick tumbled, mended, and lifted back to its original place forming the chimney once again.

Sighing in relief because let's face it, who would want to explain to their landlord how they blew up the chimney, with an ice spear. Facing Chloe, I say.

"Thanks for that. I know my gift is growing but I don't have control of it." She walks over to me hugging me from the front while Tori whacks me in the back of the head saying. "Next time you are to speak up before blowing things up. We could have tried using our connection to help you with your control, you idiot."

She is right but who wants to admit this. My stubborn brain would rather try first. "You may be right, but I need to try on my own first." Having a gift passed to you is not like the ones you are born with. Over the years my vision gift has grown but it is adaptable. Feels natural as it gets stronger and evolves.

The ice magic has been getting stronger but having ice running through my veins isn't natural yet. The cold no longer bugs me, thank the Gods.

We think when I reach 25, the ice gift will be fully developed and rooted in my soul. My aura is a mix of white light and ice blue with a swirl of what looks like wings behind me that show my species, which is Valkyrie. I can hide the swirling wings like my friends, we practiced for years before we came out of hiding.

I can still remember the cave we used to hide in. Those wet, damp walls towards the back where we could get some water in a little fresh pool that was like a spring. The dirt floor that we tried to make comfortable with some blankets we had gotten from the nearby village. The fire in the center of this is what made it even remotely warm. Sometimes we would have some animal visitors but mostly for a few years, we were on our own. Going down to the village at night to get what we needed or going hunting in the woods. Thankfully Chloe could grow the vegetables that we needed. The first year she had to go get the seeds from the gardens in the village but after that, it was like they imprinted on her and she was able to grow them without having the seeds. With Tori summoning the rain to keep them growing it seemed to be the perfect system. I just wish that I could have a more useful gift. In those days I felt useless and more of a burden.

Remembering this I knew I had to tell them about earlier when my wings popped out, but I think they have had enough surprises today that rock their world. I run my hand over the back of my head from the smack. "Shit, did you have to do that? I only have so many brain cells."

saying turning out of the hug from Chloe, giving Tori a mischievous smile. She snorted out a laugh saying. "Right because you're the brains of this operation."

We both turn to look over at Chloe who is the smartest one of us. She could have her first degree by now but now she is stuck here with us. Chloe at this point just rolls her eyes. "I think that whatever brains she does have we should try to preserve. Now we should try to have Alex touch something or someone before we head down to help Brian out."

Chloe reached forward to grab my hand. As I gripped her hand, I focused on the vision that I had earlier trying to get it to come to the surface again. The vision earlier didn't come back so I switched to just trying to look into her.

Sometimes when I look deeper into a person's soul the soul shows me things about the person or what they have done.

When nothing happened, I opened my eyes, throwing my hand up in frustration. "That didn't work, am I going to have to touch the vampire again to have it come back?" Rubbing my temples, I try to go back to myself, for the vision to tell me more but it still did nothing. There was no new information from what I already saw. "I have no more information to learn from what I already saw. It is not a good idea right now simply for the fact alone he is part of the royal court." I go on further in exasperation.

Tori turns me around to her, feeding her healing energy into me. Having her do this is like getting a hit from a joint. I immediately calm down and my shoulders relax. "Is that a little better? I think I should try something else. Don't worry this won't hurt but it might give us some more information on you. You just need to let me in." Taking a breath, I lower my guard letting her in. I would always let them in. I knew this deep in my soul to be true.

Then Tori closes her eyes, feeding her gift into me in a different way. I can feel the tendrils of her gift sweeping across my soul. After a few minutes, she retracts back from me. I no longer feel her inside of me. I put my guard back up and looked into her eyes praying she was able to find something.

Her deep brown eyes are not giving anything away. Darn, she is a good poker player. Why would this be any different? "Looking at your soul, I can tell that you have changed and you aren't done. The ice gift is very much settled into you. Your core feels naturally cold now, so that is a good sign, but your vision gift feels way different. I can't place my finger on why. This may be something we just need to see through before we have answers. Sorry." She was stern but sad at the fact that she couldn't figure me out I think but, in all honesty, some days I couldn't figure out myself.

I give her a small smile to reassure her. To break the ice, so to speak, she goes on to say. "I think that you are safe to touch other people tonight. The fact that you can't bring the vision back on your own goes to prove that the vampire is important in seeing this vision."

I shrug. "Good enough for me, but what if we run out of ice at the bar. I could do a bartender trick with ice instead of bottles." This caused the girls to laugh. We turned as one to go back downstairs.

I for one needed to change after Tori tackled me to the ground. I was a mess. Walking into my room, the other two go down to have a snack I'm sure before we start our shift.

Opening up the closet I grab a black flowy blouse that will look good over a black lace bralette. It is marginally see-through in the right light. This may get me some tips. Pulling the outfit together I grab the extra brush from my nightstand to smooth out the mess. Turning to the door I see Tori walk past with Chloe. She yells over her shoulder. "Nice! But

Brian just called and apparently there is a dress code tonight. Put that tight black dress on; that I know is hiding in the back corner of your closet."

Shit, they need to stop going in my closet.

Walking back over I huff out a "Fine" with a groan as I dig to the back corner. Thinking this can't be happening. The last time I wore this we had been in New York City at an art exhibit. We were blending in with the other chic high-class women but we were there to catch the demon who likes to eat these high-class women. Pretty gross but that was the job. Still can't believe the art gallery didn't have better security for its patrons.

They brought us in after two people had gone missing. After finding the place in the basement, where it takes its victims, we were able to use me for bait and the other two hid close by in case the demon took someone else. Unfortunately, it did take someone else but we were able to find them before she was devoured. Sending that demon back to hell was messy and he did get a good bite of me before I took his head off.

Just remembering all of this, I had a chill going up and down my spine. But I needed to get a better memory attached to this dress or I would have to throw it out and what kind of person throws out Chanel. I also normally couldn't afford this brand but the gallery paid for it.

I slip on a thong that comes to a heart at the top of my but. I take the dress off the hanger, unzipping it down the side and slipping into it. I slip my arms into the sleeves that hang down my arm off the shoulder. Zipping the dress up the side, smoothing the soft material into place, and adjusting the front so my boobs didn't fall out but still put on a good show.

Well, a tasteful show laughing to myself putting on the Jimmy Cho shoes the gallery also had purchased for me. Going over to the door with the full-length mirror standing next to it to do a quick assessment.

Pulling my hair up to a long waterfall going between my shoulder blades is a nice touch with the added benefit of keeping me cool. Leaning forward I checked my makeup that just needed a little more smokiness around the eye.

Looking up and down I finish smoothing out the length of satin going down to just above the knee hugging my small hips. I do an air kiss to myself in the mirror and walk out to the top of the stairs whistling for my friends who come running out of their rooms. Chloe tossed a shoe at Tori. "Found your other shoe!" Chloe holding her bottom lip in her top teeth gave away that she at one point stole them from Tori's closet.

Tori just flipped her the bird and kept going down the stairs behind me. It is no use trying to scold Chloe when it comes to clothes.

Grabbing an energy bar out of the cupboard. I rip it open walking to the door that leads downstairs. Realizing after I take my first bite that Chloe is wearing the necklace that I have been searching for. I try to call her out on this but instead I end up choking on my bar. Coughing in the middle of the stairs, pointing at Chloe with Tori hammering on my back I'm sure it was in a cartoon show somewhere. Aaaahhhh finally got the stupid bar down. "Hey, that is my necklace! I've been looking for that for a week!" I get this out as Tori starts to throw her hands up. Chloe winks then opens the door to end the conversation.

Shit, she is good.

She knows I will forget about this and she won't have to get yelled at again for being a closet thief. Tori looks over her shoulder saying. "Man, she is good! Just give up Alex she always will do this." I stomped my foot. Awe! Not a good idea in heels. Taking my foot out of the heeled shoe I do a quick rub before putting it back on to walk out the door.

Stepping out into the alcove I let my eyes adjust to the darkened atmosphere for the night. Taking a deep breath, I push away from the wall going down to get my orders. If all goes well tonight, I think Mr. Riley will finally give him a raise, maybe even promote him to an actual manager.

Reaching the bar, I do a scan of the area to not just find my friends but to find out who is on staff tonight. Looking at the area by the dance floor with the standing-only tables I see Carmen, Grace, and Carl who is on his second week of training. Turning to the booths and tables beyond that I see Ray serving an appetizer to a regular couple that comes in early every Friday night for the early happy hour. I thought it was cute how they always seemed to be able to make the rest of us disappear.

My smile faded away as it landed on Agatha and Jade with their lapdog Trever following them around, hoping for scraps. They usually tend to the standing tables for they aren't good with being personable and let>s face it being nice in general.

My first run-in with those three was about a year ago when Jade started working here first. She put a very good act on for them, to then hire Agatha a few short weeks later. After they were both working here, the trouble started.

Some of the crap they pull is stealing tips off of other wait staff tables, tripping other wait staff to get them demoted to a smaller section, or even trying to get behind the bar to try getting one of the bartending spots. After a couple of months of doing things like this, they got a warning from Brian that if they didn't stop this, then he would bring it up to Mr. Riley.

Things cooled down for a bit but lately ever since Trever started two months ago, they have been trying a few more of their tricks. The thing is they never went too far so they wouldn't get fired. They also did it in a way that you have to question if it was them or someone else.

This was the most popular and nicest bar on the east side. All the people who came here are high tippers and high class. Not to mention our owner doesn't just own this building but most of the block. He has been leaving things to Brian more and more these days. We think he is getting more involved with politics or he got a new land deal to develop.

The amount of time he spends in fancy suits and meetings has gone up in the last few months. We tried to ask him about it but he just smiled. It is nothing important yet. Which means he is working on something big.

Mr. Riley is not just a business entrepreneur but the kindest man who never shorts his employees or treats you like crap.

He has blue eyes with a smile ready for a good laugh or when he is doing business, he can catch bullshit from a mile away. His hair is thick, steel grey, cut short, parted off to one side. He has a tall frame with muscles that still have the women coming around. His stride has a small limp from a few years back when he still broke up bar fights. But now it just adds to his charm.

We met him when we came to the area at eighteen looking for jobs and a place to live. He gave us our first job that eventually led to him helping us start our business called Hunter>s. He helped us get it started and still likes to be kept in the loop about what we are up to. He even bailed us out once when a demon got a grip of Chloe, he used his lightning gift to help distract him while we took out the demon. The three of us call him Ry, he is a surrogate uncle or father that we no longer have. Even though he is in his mid-forties.

Think of the devil and he shall appear. Ry stroll's in wearing a fancy three-piece suit. I can't help but whistle at him. He turns in my direction with a smile and a wink. He then does the fashion walk over to me with the three-point turn and strikes a pose.

"Well, Ry I have to say you look hot with the right amount of class. What's the occasion?" I say framing him in with my hands at different angles. "Well, those big shots that are coming in are expecting me to be here. I thought I might as well look the part of a businessman for the night," he says with a lopsided grin. "Well, in that case before you are in that role I think I'll get my hug now." Leaning in, wrapping my arms around his middle. He kisses the top of my head saying. "Good idea. Where are my other two Hunters at?" Laughing, I look over his shoulder to see them coming from around the bar. "Well, you're in luck, I think they are headed over here." Ry shifts to look over his shoulder at them coming. His smile gets wider as they approach. Turning full around with his arm still draped around my shoulders he says. "Looks like we got the dress code right for tonight. You all look beautiful." Chloe Blushed to reach forward to hug him around the middle. Tori did the same before sitting on a barstool.

"So, who are these big shots that we are all dolled up for?" Tori asks, cocking one eyebrow up.

Ry looks around before speaking. "We need to head up that way, I can fill you in while I show you girls what needs to be done." He turns to walk away from us knowing we will follow. Before he can get halfway there Agatha and Jade just happen to be in that area bussing a table. Seeing them coming up to him was like a cat stalking its prey. I motion for us to stop a foot back to watch this play out.

Jade comes around the table to his right and Agatha leans on the table flicking her fake blond hair over her shoulder giving Ry the best impression of an innocent girl. Haha yeah, that isn't going to work sister. Jade reaches for his arm linking their arms together like he is escorting her to prom. She beams her overly filled lips up at him with a wink. These girls are laying this on thick. I have to bite my lower lip from laughing out loud. Ry hated scenes.

Jade was the first one of them to speak. "Hi, Mr. Riley! Or should we call you Ry now since we have been here so long?" She asks, squeezing closer to him." Yes, that does seem like a good idea!" Agatha pipes up. Without letting him reply she adds. "You know what else is a great idea, moving us up to being bartenders, or better yet I would like to put my name down to manage this place. You're so busy with your other businesses I bet you could use the help. I am a well-respected and trusted member of the staff." She says this with her arm sliding through his other arm. They even go as far as trying to get him to walk with them for two steps before he can politely free himself from their claws.

He steps a foot back causing them to turn to face him. Thank the Gods, he does know we get to see their faces when he turns them down, or better yet, please fire them. I cross my fingers behind my back. Praying for this to happen.

Tori is hiding her mouth behind her hand to cover the small laugh that escapes at their shocked face at him pulling away. Chloe holds my other hand so tight I think she may break something.

We are still in the range to hear Ry's reply. Clearing his throat, he says "It is nice to see you girls, but don't call me Ry. You may, like always, call me Mr. Riley. As for bartending, we are already full up for those jobs, and waitressing is where you are needed. The management position that is rumored to be happening, is going to Brian. I just told him and he will be announcing this to you himself, if you could please go over to the bar area for the final briefing for the night. I hope you have a great shift, now if you excuse me, I need to show Alex, Chloe, and Tori what they will be doing in the VIP section tonight."

Putting his hand up to stop Jade from speaking, almost made me cheer. With his voice now towards the impatient side, I could hear the edge of anger coming through, at how they are treating him and how they are asking for the job promotions. "Before you volunteer to help them, you are not needed. You don't have the right finesse that is required for the group of people that are coming tonight. So, you ladies have a great night." He says this and turns around giving us an eye roll and points to the stairs.

Their faces are pure furry and loathing for us, as we wave walking after him. I can't help but smile, shaking my head at their gumption. They seem to be under the impression that if they slut it up, then everything will be handed to them. Not going to happen ladies. You need to do the work and not be a bitch.

Getting up to the VIP area I notice that the decor has been changed to deep reds and velvety black accents. The taller tables near the ledge are wrapped in silk black tablecloths with deep dark red plates and black chrome silverware. Moving to the smaller tables I see they are in dark red tablecloths with a black overlay of sheer black crackled looking material. The plates are matte black with black chrome silverware. The large table at the center is in black silk cloth with a sheer silver starry night material. Making it look like the night sky from my dreams. The plates were silver with the same black chrome silverware as the others. Every table had a low crystal vase with the deepest red roses I had ever seen. The napkins were silk black folded with little menus poking out of them. The menus were on thick white rustic paper with deep red lettering. To complete the look there are crystal jewels scattered with rose petals on the tables. These were important people if Ry went to all this trouble of redecorating the VIP area.

I wonder how he knew that he not only was hosting it but invited. Maybe we will be able to see what he has been up to with his time finally.

Looking off to the left I see that the private bar was set up with crystal as well and that there were tall crystal vases at either end with Black roses and red gems in the water as the ascent. I just whistle. "Fwheeoo" tilting my head giving the room one last sweep. "Ok after seeing this my birthday party may change a little," I whisper to Chloe. She reaches up pulling me by the ear. "Ouch!" I say in protest. Rubbing my ear. "As we could ever pull something like this off." She sighs then says. "Besides, you're lucky. We love your smart ass! You're a lot of work." Tori just points at Chloe saying. "Yeah and besides, what is wrong with our traditional cheap champagne and pizza spread?"

Looking around again I can't disagree. I love those traditions. "You have me there. I guess you will just have to do this when we hit it big." I say laughing. Ry comes out of the back room with some crystal cantors that are filled with a thick red liquid. Placing it on the bar with a careful hand.

He had all our attention.

Sitting down in front of him I look at him but then realize what this was. Blood! Yep, that is blood. Covering my mouth, my eyes are wide with shock and I just can't believe that this was here.

We never served blood to our patrons. Vampires can still drink alcohol but it doesn't do much to them through affecting their blood alcohol level like in humans. Supernatural's are affected by alcohol but have a higher tolerance than humans. Blood is not something that we can serve out of the tap and it can be more costly for those who aren't in the Vampire section of the town. They have a facility that makes synthetic blood but still takes donations from willing patrons at their blood banks.

"I can see by your face Alex that you are surprised to see this here. You should be, but listen up no one is to know that we have this up here. This blood was brought here for this occasion by the court's approval. Furthermore, this is to be kept at slightly above room temperature in these dispensers under the counter to your right. On the left, some dispensers are slightly colder for the ones who prefer it chilled. Below the bar, special warmers are set up with dispensers for the different types of blood that are being provided. I will warn you if you cut yourself tonight then your blood will be more appetizing than this back here.

You will become a target for every vampire that is coming tonight. Fresh blood from the vein will always be more appetizing. Be careful and never offer your neck to one of them." He explains with a firm voice.

My head is reeling from everything he just said. "I can understand now, why you were so cryptic about who was coming but even when vampires come here, you never serve blood. Why now? How important are they?" I ask. He gently takes my hand, giving it a light squeeze. "You›re right, I never do this but these folks are some of the highest-ranking of the court. Some may even be the royals themselves. I don't know the exact names of those coming tonight because they don't want to draw attention to themselves.

So keep an open mind about tonight and remember to always be on point for the head table." He stresses this with a nod toward the silvery night table. Tori speaks up. "Are we going to start serving blood regularly or is this a one-night thing for this event?" Yeah, that is a good question for this will change the patrons some. I wonder if the vampires are going to start mingling with the other races now. Ry answered, rubbing the back of his neck. "I honestly don't know. If they do decide to start mixing with the races more, then yes, blood will become a part of our menu for those of that race." That's good enough an answer for me so I decide to move on. "What are the food options then tonight if they normally don't need to eat food, why are the plates out?" I ask, waving at the table nearest to me.

"That is something else I need to tell you about. There are some desserts made of blood. These items are served warm and cold. There is a blood chocolate cake and blood ice cream. You will be presenting them at different times. The blood chocolate cake is to be served first at 8 o'clock and the blood ice cream is at 10 o'clock. In between this, you will be getting them alcohol or blood beverages. The deserts are in the back. I thought you could come early to prepare ahead of time. I believe we should have thirty coming but we should be prepared for forty." He says taking a look at us before motioning for us to get to the back to start preparing the desserts.

We all got up but I decided to hang back a little. I watch them walk back giving me odd looks. I shake my head and smile at them.

Turning back to Ry seeing the stress in his eyes, I reach over the back taking his face in my right palm. "Hey, are you good? Don't lie to me." I say looking hard into his eyes. He places his hand over mine responding. "I will be. Don't worry about this old man. I will be better when we sit down after tonight and have one of those mojitos you love." Laughing at him I pull my hand free. "That, you can bet on. I'm guessing you>re not manning the bar so get out from behind before you get something on yourself." I cock my thumb, gesturing to the side.

He tries to look all innocent but I don't think he can ever get away with it. "Ok yeah, good idea. Brian will be up shortly to give you girls a hand. I'll be at the head table, so if you need anything, whisper in my ear or pass me a note." With this, he gives me one last smile before heading out.

I looked after him, thinking something was up. We will eventually figure it out but until then better just go with the flow.

Going through the door behind the bar, I can see that they are hard at work with Brian getting the deserts at least in the stone bowls and plates glazed in a midnight black with silver swirling throughout.

I take some of the finished ones and place them on a tray that will go on a rack to be stored in the walk-in freezer or the sub-zero refrigerator. Looking more closely at the ice cream I can see that it is thick like a ganache and the color is a deep red that reminds me of a velvet comforter. It looks delicious. I shake my head smiling to myself at my thoughts. I can't believe I almost tasted some

Brian finishes cutting the cake and decides to go behind the bar to take inventory and log some of the numbers into the computer upfront. This allows us to finally speak, without anyone around.

Immediately, Tori says. "Shit, what are we going to do if your guy from this morning shows up? You said he is in the royal court. They like to keep a low profile." Yep, she is right, if he does, I would have to explain things and he would know where I work, possibly live, if he asks or reads Ry's mind. "If that happens, then I will avoid the head table. I'm sure that's where the royal court will be sitting. I'll just let you know if he shows up. Until then I will try to chill." I say adjusting my shoulders like getting ready for a fight.

They both nod, giving each other a worried look. "Hey! Don't worry," I said. "Even if he does, I can handle him." I hope that sounded more confident than I feel. I finish putting the trays on the racks for them to wheel back into the freezer or sub-zero refrigerator.

Walking back over to the counter I ever so gracefully hoist myself up to rest my feet before this night gets going. Tori and Chloe come over on either side of me to do the same.

Leaning my head on Chloe, the shorty in the group was natural and she rested on my shoulder in the meantime. Brian walks in on his phone but quickly holds it up taking a picture of the three of us. "Hey! Wait, we aren't ready for our debut." Saying holding my hand up to my forehead to add some drama. Brain laughs, shaking his head. "Before and after shots. Let's see how you fare on those heels tonight. Remember, breaking your neck will not get you out of clean up." He says wagging his eyebrows.

Tori throws a dishrag at him and jumps down to finish the job when it didn't even make it partway. Backing up Brian yells "Mercy! Mercy!" Tori goes in for the kill shot as she gets right at that spot, on his right side where he is the most ticklish.

Hopping down with Chloe we grab his phone to see if it is an acceptable picture because you can never trust a guy to have that kind of judgment.

Seeing that it is a good picture, I call out to Tori who is now on the defense, for Brian has her wrapped up tickling her on the stomach. "Ok, Ok you two that's enough! Boss man is going to come back and he is already stressed out. Tori, go straighten yourself out before someone sees you." They break apart still laughing like loons. Tori stumbles off to the back where there is a small bathroom.

Brian catches the phone that Chloe tosses at him. He walks back through the door to the balcony but comes right back in. "They are starting to arrive. Get out there and take your spots." He says in a rush before his head pops out of sight again. Well, this is it. I can do this.

CHAPTER 7

S tanding behind the bar I can see that Ry had put up a shield to keep all sound out and those down below couldn't see up here but we could still see them. I loved that trick but we didn't do that often, it got expensive.

None of us had the gift to make shields and besides it would get tiring holding one up that long. Judging by the sparkle of the shield, it was made by one of Freya's charms.

She loved to add a bit of sparkle here and there.

I reached down for Brian's hand and squeezed it before moving down the bar to make myself more available. The first few that came through the curtain had the paler complexion to their brown skin. Their eyes flashed around the room going slightly red for a second before moving to one of the high-top tables by the ledge of the balcony. That was a little off-putting but they are still staggeringly beautiful. Even the men could be called beautiful.

Tori gave them a couple of seconds to take their seats before approaching them. Chloe was getting some of the drink orders, from the lower smaller tables.

The Head table remained empty at this point. I wonder if they are planning on making one of those royal big entrances when they get their name and station called out before entering.

I giggle to myself looking down but as I look back up, I realize that a guy is sitting at the bar in front of me. I quickly place a smile on my face and see that he is at least smiling too. And perk, his fangs were not completely out. He has grey eyes that speak of danger and Black hair that is swept back from his chiseled perfect face that could have been done by Michelangelo. His muscular body could still be seen through the suit that was unbuttoned to show off a little bit of hair that came out of the top. His smile was just as lethal as his eyes peeling back more as his fangs lengthen somewhat.

As I come forward to ask him if he requires anything I feel pressure on my brain. I wince, stepping back from the man in front of me. Grabbing the ledge of the counter behind to stabilize before I say. "Oye, stop it! That shit doesn't work on me!" Brian heard me and came over to address the man but I put my hand up to stop him. I can handle this guy. I feel the pressure recede.

The guy looked perplexed at the fact that he couldn't get into my head. I step back over saying. "Now that you have tried that, can I ask you what you would like to drink this evening?" He frowned at me, saying. "Yes, I did try but what are you, that you can resist the pull on your mind? How about instead of a drink, you take your break and go someplace a little more private." He reaches for my hand but another man comes with blonde hair and a scar going down his left cheek comes over, slapping his hand down on his shoulder. "I see you have found a lovely barmaid to play with but don't you think she is better where she is than off with you in the corner.

Our brother will be here soon and you know how he likes it when you behave yourself, Mason." He says this last bit a little under his breath but I could still hear him. He holds his other hand out offering it to me. "Hi, I'm Eric, the other brother to the future king. I would like to apologize for my young brother here." I put my hand in his and I see a flash of a sword coming down slicing through his cheek. He stumbles back from his attacker swiping back with his sword, taking the man at the neck. After the man falls the vision fades away.

I come fully back into myself. Blinking a few times to clear my head. During this, I can respond and stay present, thankfully. "Hi, I'm Alex and yes I would be more useful tonight serving drinks. What can I get for you gentleman?" Stepping back, I grab crystal Bordeaux wine glasses. They both look at me like I did something out of character. I think they noticed my green eyes cloud slightly. This usually happens when I go into a vision. Usually, people don't notice this but vampires have heightened senses.

Crap they knew something was off about me.

After a beat, Eric interjected before Mason could say anything more. Judging by the frown and rib jab Eric reserved this was not what he wanted to ask. "We would like type A- warm. Can you bring that over to the head table? Thanks" He says in a hurry, taking Mason at the back of the neck and I think applying some pressure to get him to move. As they move away, I walk over to Brian who has been covering the drink tickets. For he is using some speed tonight to keep up with the orders. Wow, he may have to get thicker souls on those shoes or he will wear them out before the night is over.

I grab the two A- passing them off to Tori giving her a nod at the two gentlemen at the head table to where they need to go. Then getting back to helping Brian with the others that are now coming to the bar directly from the entrance instead of finding their tables.

A few times I felt some pressure on my brain but that didn't slow me down. The only thing that slowed me down was when a woman with dark brown curls who didn't get my attention fast enough decided to levitate a glass in front of my face.

That startled me.

Laughing, I turned to her. "That was an original way to cut ahead of the line. What can I get you for your trouble?" She leans forward to say. "Why thank you for asking. I would love a glass of chilled B+." Her mischievous smile was one of pure gold that the woman next to her that has short blonde hair I think did not appreciate as she then grabbed the drink, I was handing to the curly hair mischievous Vampire.

On seeing a catfight about to happen in front of me I quickly took a drink that was coming from the same tap and gave it to Miss. Mischievous winking at her. She rolled her eyes bumping into the blonde as she got up causing blondie to spill her drink down the front of her dress. Thankfully it is black and will hide the beverage but let's face it there is a cardinal rule. Like, don't mess with a woman's drink. That usually applied to the things like the date rape drug or putting rum instead of whiskey in her drink but I guess stealing a drink or spilling her drink on a said female would count.

The blonde erupted from her seat turning around finding the mischievous girl gone already. She stomps off to the private restrooms in the VIP area. I walk around the bar to clean up the small mess.

Never thought I would be cleaning up blood at a cocktail party. Laughing to myself as I did.

After wiping the chair, I realized that some had gotten on the floor as well. Sighing, I bend my knees off to the side, lowering myself down onto my toes.

I feel a hand under my arm. Looking up I find that it is the first vampire I met at the bar. Mason, I believe is his name. He gives me a slow tug up causing me to stumble back into him. He has his arm around my waist and his hand over my mouth. In a flash pulling me into the shadows of the alcove at the end of the bar. He quickly turns me around up against the wall holding me in place with most of his body. With the music so loud I'm sure no one would hear me.

Looking up into his face I see that his fangs are fully out. He is pushing my head off to the side to get a better angle of my neck. The feel of his tongue running up the side of my neck makes me shutter. I feel him kiss just below my earlobe before he bites down on it. "Aaahhhh!" I scream into his hand. He laughs into my ear. "Haha, yes that pulse is going. Did you know the blood always tastes better when the pulse is higher? I think we can take this somewhere else and get it even higher but I may wreck this nice dress." I can feel him hardening up against my stomach pressing me into the wall.

I want to gag now.

Suddenly I feel his weight come off of me. I hear him hiss in protest, as a man in a dark suit pins him to the other wall of the alcove. "What the fuck are you doing brother, have you no control? We are not in the right place for this. This event is for business. I am to be King shortly and I need to get the rest of the council on my side, so for the rest of the night you are to be in the company of Eric." He growls this out with the venom to back it up. Backing away he releases his brother. "Fine, but take a whiff of her then tell me how I am supposed to resist her. She is different." He desperately gets out before walking out of the alcove.

Shit! He can smell that I am different? Not good!

I slowly shift to walk away from the soon-to-be King. His hand slaps the wall forcing me to stop my exit. He leans into me, backing me up into the wall once more. "Let me go. I don't know what he is talking about. I just work here." I say pushing on his chest. "I believe my brother is right. I don't know why you smell more appetizing. I had to restrain myself earlier but now that I have you again, I don't think I will." Hearing him say this, I finally lookup. I gasp at seeing Lucas standing over me. "You're the Crown Prince! This morning you pretended to be Patrol? Did you even tell them about the demon I killed?" I ask, astonished at this man holding me in place.

Looking into his face with his arms on either side of me. It just felt right to be in his arms. Why his arms felt this way is beyond me. I wanted to get him away from me but at the same time, I wanted to pull him in closer. Almost like he read my thoughts this time he lowered his head, grazing his lips across my cheekbone. This sends tingles up my spine and I wiggle under his grasp getting closer. I let out another gasp as his hand moved up to my ponytail tugging it making my head go back. "Wait this can't be happening. I need to stay away from you. Let me go." This comes out in a hoarse voice. Opening my eyes I see that his eyes are rimmed in red and his fangs are extended.

"I think that this is not over Alex. This is the second time in one day that we are on the same path. I will regretfully let you go, for now." He says, releasing my hair that he had twined around his fist. As his hand slides down my arm, I feel the pull of the vision.

I am again back on the dock. Looking at my surroundings I remember that last time the men were loading up the ship. I peered around the crate seeing that they were again loading up the ship. The last time the skeleton guy could see me.

I wonder if these men could see me now or was it just that one time.

I slowly get out from behind the crate hurrying towards the men. Calling out. "Hi, you need to get out of here! A man with a small army of demons is coming. I have seen you all die in a vision. Please get out of here." The one called Godrick turns around. Covering his eyes he says. "Cover thee self. You shouldn't be out here in your nightclothes." I look down seeing that I am in the same dress as I am wearing in the present time.

I grab a ruff cloth from the nearby crate and rush the rest of the way to them. "We don't have much time! Godrick you and your men will be killed tonight if you don't heed my warning. My gift is visions of the past and future. I have been in this past before and seen you all die." I try to say with a level voice but I know I sound a bit off. Sven comes up to Godrick placing his hand on his shoulder. "If this is true then let's depart with the tide going out. We can come back for this when the coast is clear. If she is right, I am not ready to die today." He says this and turns to get up on the ship. Godrick grunts. "I will heed this warning for you. I have to urge you to come with us. We cannot leave you here unattended and unarmed to fight alone." I have no idea when this vision is going to end and I don't want to be taken by the skeleton guy and his demons. Godrick offers me his hand going up the gangplank. The two cast off and Sven goes to the sail, opening it up to catch the breeze that will carry us out of here.

I hurry to the rail looking up the hill waiting for them to arrive. When I see the first black figure followed by many more I yell out. "Hurry, they are coming!" I feel a pull from the boat as they use the rowers to get some momentum. We are now ten feet away from the dock but I hear the thunder with the lightning not far behind.

I feel a pull of cold from deep inside myself. With the urge to let it come out. No idea why this is suddenly happening but trusting my instincts with my gift has always proven to be the right way to go. I throw my hands up, picturing a wall of ice. The cold that I keep at bay rises to the surface. I can feel the ice as it explodes out of my hands. Creating essentially a tall glacier wall bobbing in the water. I keep feeding it more of my gift but it is draining. I feel the first bolt of lightning that hits the top of the iceberg. Shards of the iceberg break off falling in the ocean creating waves. I fall on the deck when one of the stronger waves tips the boat to the right. Some of the residual ice in me creeps across the deck, icing it over. I gasp, scrambling up and running to the side again to continue replenishing the wall. The men behind me are hard at work and don't notice when I start to fade going back to my own time.

I call out to them but nothing comes out. I can hear this deep voice calling to me to come back. To wake up. "You need to come back." The gravely deep voice said. I felt a little dizzy and as I tried to open my eyes the room spun.

This is reminding me of the margarita night we had last year on Cinco De Mayo. The room was spinning in the same direction as last time but at least I didn't feel sick. Blinking a few more times brought the face above me into focus. I jump pushing on the rock-hard chest of the one and only, Lucas. I start to sit up but am held firmly in place in the man's lap on the floor of the back room. How did I get back here? My mind started to catch up to my body as I could now hear my friends trying to get to me but were held back by several guards. I could see that Tori was about to unleash a storm by the way her hair was blowing by an unforeseen wind that she created. Chloe and Brian were arguing with Mason and Eric who kept them from getting through to me.

Ry was pacing back and forth with the sound of thunder following him with every step. The lightning was visibly running up and down his arms. No one approached him for fear of getting electrocuted, I'm sure.

I shake my head at all the voices around me and focus on the man above me again. One of his hands brushed some stray hairs that escaped from my ponytail out of my face and then ran his fingers along my jawline coming to rest at my chin. He moves my head back and forth looking intently at my face.

That simple act made me want to curl up on his lap like a cat and purr.

I swallow, closing my eyes before looking up at him, placing my hand on his chest I say. "I had another vision? I wasn't able to stay present again?" He nodded his head saying. "Yes" I try to take a deep breath but it comes out shaky. Instead, I respond by trying not to have a shake in my voice. "Thank you for catching me but can you please tell me why my friends are being held back from me and why you are not letting me up?" He slowly put me in a sitting position on his lap but still didn't let me up. "I think you should stay right where you are until I think you can stand without falling. I kept your friends back because you started to fade. I believe your vision was trying to take you fully to where it was taking place. I was able to anchor you here by entering your mind. You let me in this time and I was able to hold onto you" After a beat of waiting for me to reply he says...

"Judging by your shocked face this is new for you." He says this all while playing with my fingers on my lap.

Ry came closer bending down, taking my face in his hands looking deep into my eyes. I look back into his eyes touching his cheek, I say. "I'm fine Ry. Really. It is just new; you know me I can handle anything. "He let go of my face but pulled me up by the hand that had caressed his cheek. I am pulled into a bone-crushing hug. "You should have told me that your gifts had started to change. You know I can help. I'm always here for you." The reassurance from him almost brought me to tears.

I pulled back looking at my friends that had finally stopped arguing and fighting with the guards now that I was upright. I looked back at the now-standing Lucas. I point at my friends arching one eyebrow, indicating that I thought that this was overkill. He shrugged, waving my friends forward. His guards stepped aside as my friends charged forward, engulfing me in a hug.

Tori started on me first. "What the hell happened and why are you in the arms of the soon-to-be king?" Chloe said "Yes! Answer that now!" With Brian saying. "Are you sure you're ok?" He put his arm around me pulling me into him.

I hear a growl from the man behind me. I look back to see Lucas stalking forward. He pulls me free from Brian's side hug placing one hand on my waist and the other on my hip. What the hell! I'm not the only shocked person either.

Eric steps closer, eyeing his brother cautiously. "Brother! The man is her friend, he will not hurt her. I feel no malice coming from him." He comes forward all the way to stand in front of me looking his brother in the eyes. "You can let her go, no one will harm her here." Eric steps back.

I feel his hand on my arm tighten before he fully releases me. I immediately turned around staring up into his face. His face looks pained and that frown is back from this morning. I square my shoulders. "What is going on, first you withhold me from my friends, then you don't let me get up from your lap when I was clearly recovered and lastly you grab me from my friend when he is giving me a hug," I say at this point I am in full defense mode.

If he grabs me again, I will punch him.

He takes a step in my direction but I take a step back trying to keep the distance between us. He stops, rubbing his hand over his face. "I didn't know how to explain it this morning. I could feel something different about you. I think with all the rain coming down your scent was diluted but now I can smell you and sense you more. Your body's calling to me." He says, taking another step to me.

"I also think your vision has something to do with me. Each time we have been together your gift has sent you into a vision." Shit, he is figuring this out way too quickly.

I turn to my friends pleading with them to say something. Chloe steps by me patting my arm. "I think we all need to go someplace a little more private for this conversation and also there are a lot of people out there waiting for their desserts. I would like to offer a compromise. Alex is fine now. We will continue with this evening and talk about this tomorrow or later tonight." She suggests.

Ry comes forward. "I think this is a wise choice. It took a lot to get your fellow vampires out of their side of town. If we want them to agree with the business plan we will need to go forward." Ry moves aside indicating that they should go out to the party once more.

Lucas steps to me, taking my arm. "I will be taking the tonight option. We will be moving up the timetable for the desserts and I will give this another 2 hour. After that, we are going to talk." This was more of a command than a suggestion of the events that will be happening tonight.

His brother Eric walks to where Mason is leaning on the wall. They talk briefly before going out onto the balcony. "I agree, if this is that important then we could continue with the evening. I will talk to you afterward but I have questions of my own that you have to answer." I say. Looking up into his face again, I can see that he is fighting with something mentally. He inclines his head to the side. "Yes, I suspected as much. I think you downplayed your vision this morning." This statement was eerie. He and Ry walk out the door together with the guards following behind.

Turning to my friends I can see that they are going to beat me with questions and they know how to get them out of me. I walk up to them propping my hip on the counter I say. "Ok let's get to work. We can figure out my gift later." They didn't look happy with me. "Fine, we will do this your way as long as you are sure you're ok," Chloe says looking up into my face.

She may be short but man she can still be intimidating. I squeeze the so-called sauce on the cake. "I'm fine, a little shook up but fine." This gets the girls moving but not happily. "Ok, it is a good idea to keep this going but come on, you know this is not good. That vampire was looking at you like you are a piece of meat or his toy that he doesn't want to share. Don't get me started on the brother in the corner. He was looking at you the same way but he was different somehow." Tori said. I blew out a breath answering her statement. "That would be Mason and he grabbed me when I was cleaning up some blood after these two girls had a catfight. He was going to take a bite out of me until Lucas intervened. That's when I had my vision."

I duck my head leaving out the fact that he too wanted to drink from me. With him, this didn't bother me.

At the thought of him biting me a shiver went up to my spine.

CHAPTER 8

I don't know how we got through those desserts and final drinks. After we had cleared the tables we were all excused for they had to discuss things that are not ok for our ears.

This made me want to stay even more.

I waved to Brian as he was going downstairs to check on the bar and we three were going upstairs to change. I for one needed to put my feet up. Maybe take a shower. I was making the debate when Tori was grabbed from behind coming through the door. Hearing her yell was heart-stopping.

I dropped the heels that I was carrying on the stairs. Jumping down to the open door I see that it is Kyro Industries men standing there with Tori in the muscle dudes arms. The knife at her throat sent me over the edge.

Stepping forward with Chloe off to my left I call my ice to the surface forming an ice dagger. Yep, that is new. "Let her go or you will not survive this night!" I say this with a deadly calm. The guy with the greasy hair steps forward. "Your friend is not going to be harmed as long as we can agree on the job that was offered earlier. I for one don't like that we can't find any information on you three and the fact that you will not let some of Mr. Loriek's men with you, might mean you will take the stolen experiment for yourself. So, to get this job, you will be taking a blood oath or we simply have a few of our men come with you."

This was a big problem. A blood oath is a serious thing that can link two people together until the deed is done or one of them is killed. If we take the blood oath, they may be able to figure out what we are. I don't want to be their next experiment.

I eye the man in front of me. Pointing the ice dagger at him I say. "Like hell, we aren't going to take a blood oath. We are not dumb. The reason you can't find any personal information is we are private people. We will have to pass on the job. Threats and ultimatums don't work for us. Tori, come on." She pushed the arm away, then head-butted him, breaking the guy's nose.

He drops the knife and stumbles back from holding his nose. No one moves to stop her from walking away. I guess looking at their buddy gave them a chance to reassess the situation. "Ok, I do believe our business is concluded. You know the way out. Unless you guys want to go a few rounds, I can always use the exercise." I say taking my stance getting into a fight mode.

Two of the other guards pick up their fallen comrade while the greasy hair guy backs up. He throws us a card that lands at my feet. "If you want to take our terms then give us a call, but don't forget we are a powerful company. We can make life very difficult for you." With that, he turns walking to the stairway down the hallway.

I pick up the card reading the name. I finally know who this guy is, Julian Gartor. That name didn't sound threatening at all, but that guy wasn't the one to carry out a beating. No, he would get his guards or goons to do that.

Turning to Tori I see that Chloe is already taking a look at her head. "Yeah, that will hurt for a little bit but your healing gift should take care of that in no time," she says going back through the door.

Shutting the door behind us I lean over picking up my Jimmy Choo's. Looking at the ice dagger still in my hand I can't help but think a week ago I would have never been able to create something intricate and stable. My gift over ice felt more stable and the cold wasn't cold to me anymore. I felt settled. I wonder if that vision was also a way for my gift to get settled within me fully. It became stronger in the last few days.

Stepping into our apartment I hear Tori say. "Shit" as the ice pack touches her head. "Chloe why the hell do I need that? I will be fine in a few minutes." She says tensely. Chloe huffs but walks away with the ice pack roughly shoving it back into the freezer.

Leaning on the counter I hold up the dagger to them. "Ok stop, don>t start anything up I am not in the mood to clean up after you two destroy the apartment! We need to go over what the hell just happened." Chloe stepped forward, taking the dagger from me. Turning it over in her hand I could see the wheels going round and round. "You have never been able to create something like this before. How did you do this?" Her asking got me talking about the vision first.

"Let's start with the vision. I think it has something to do with this." Pointing to the dagger. "When I was pulled into that vision, I was able to talk to the men this time. I warned them about what was coming and they invited me to go with them.

I didn't know how long the vision was going to last.

I couldn't feel my body anymore.

After we got the boat moving the same hoard of demons showed up with that skeleton tattoo guy. I was able to build a wall of ice that they couldn't get through. It was tiring but I was able to do it. Something inside me pulled me to use my ice gift. To draw the cold to the surface.

The ice and cold felt more natural after I was pulled in by the vision. When those guys grabbed Tori, I barely thought about it. I just let the cold rise to the surface and pictured a dagger. It grew from my hand before I could even register what I just did." I say placing both of my hands on the counter bracing myself.

Chloe hands it over to Tori to examine. "It feels like glass, there is no way for anyone else to fight with this. Look in my hand it is starting to melt." she reaches for me, putting it in my hand. I immediately feel the slick surface refreeze. It also feels like it is slightly stuck to my hand.

"I think the vision helped anchor the ice gift inside me. I will have to do some more testing but I think my other gifts are going to help out the other ones till they are all stable in me." Thinking out loud to them was second nature. Chloe nodded her head saying. "I do believe you are right. Though I think we should go to the library to look some of this up." I nod my head. Shifting my weight back and forth I then realize that Lucas wasn't there again. "Hey, guys Lucas was still not in my vision. But during it, I could feel him and I heard him calling me back." I look to either of them to come up with an explanation. "That still doesn't sound like your usual visions. You're sure he wasn't there?" Chloe askes wrinkling her nose up as she thinks. "Yes, I don't think I could have missed him," I say, turning around as I start to pace. I may need to go back into the vision to try to find him or maybe we can find out more at the library. There had to have been someone, at some point, with my abilities.

Tori then spoke up. "Ok, I know what you are thinking and we will find out more about what is going on with you but in the meantime, we need to talk about the job that we no longer have. I don't like how that went down. There is no way we would agree with any of that but let›s face it we do need the money." Shit, she is right. I guess we will have to take one of the jobs the government gives out. Sure, those are guaranteed jobs but they pay a whole lot less. Aauuuggghh this sucks!

"I'll look at the jobs they sent us tomorrow. Right know I need to get this dress off." Walking to the stairs, I see they have the same idea. Looking over my shoulder at Tori I decide to poke the bear some. "So, you are going to put some other clothes on right? I mean the birthday suit might get you a different job altogether." Laughing, I duck as a shoe is thrown at my head.

Running up the last few steps I turn into my room, shutting my door just in time for the other shoe to hit my door. Shaking my head, I turned around to my closet praying there were some decent sweatpants for meeting with a vampire crown prince. Tapping my foot I look over at my favorite comfy leggings. Yep, that will have to do for I guess sweatpants are out. As I turn around I see myself in the full-length mirror over by the door. Stopping I ran my hand over the spot Lucas's lips had grazed. It is like they were still there. I walk closer to the mirror inspecting my cheek. I see nothing out of the ordinary but the feeling of his lips isn't the only thing I can still feel. Taking off the dress I looked at the skin on my back where his hand had been. I swear the skin is slightly a bit pink. I close my eyes, taking a deep breath. Taking one last look in the mirror before going over to pull the black leggings on. Mmm.... yeah, they feel like butter. Pulling on a pink bralette with a soft grey off-the-shoulder sweater that goes halfway to my knees. Letting my hair loose from the ponytail I can feel my scalp say aaah-hhhh. Going to the door running my fingers through my hair I call out. "Ok guys we can't get ready for bed yet we still have to meet with Ry and the crown prince tonight."

Chloe pops her head out of the bedroom at the end of the hall. "What do you take us for? Of course, we will dress up-down for them. Hey, have you seen my teal V-neck t-shirt?" She comes out of her room in some jeggings and a blue bra. Swaying her hips, she comes to Tori's door asking the same question. I walk over to the dryer. Poke my hand in pulling out the teal shirt. "Yeah, I did a load yesterday. That reminds me I have to get this demon blood and mud out of my shoes and pullover. Do you guys have anything gross that needs to be washed?" I pour some detergent in and Tori brings over a few pairs of pants she wore when working on the Mustang earlier this week. After starting that, I went downstairs to get a drink.

The easiest thing to grab was Tori's sweet red wine out of the fridge. Not my go-to but easier than making a mojito. After getting it out I see the others coming down so I get our two more wine glasses. We grabbed them with a package of Oreos and took them to the couches.

Let's face it, Oreos are made for this kind of thing.

The couch felt amazing! Sitting back into the soft old cushions was like sinking into an old friend. Propping my feet up on the coffee table with my blue fuzzy blanket was pure heaven. The others did the same with Tori diving into the Oreos first. Looking at her I switch hands, snapping my fingers for a cookie. She didn't even miss a beat. She tossed it to me not even looking at where my hand was. Landing in my hand dead center. Shit, she is good!

After we all had a few cookies, I finally got the gumption to talk. "The side glances are not going to get you the information you guys want. Just ask me already." Chloe smirked, rolling her eyes at the ceiling. "Well now that you put it that way. Yes, I want to know if Lucas can be trusted and why he says you smell different. We are the same species. Do Tori and I also smell different to them?" God's above, she makes a good point. Running my free hand through my hair racking my nails on my scalp as I go through it. I just groaned out of my frustration. " You know what, I was getting a weird vibe all night. Sometimes I swear some of those Vampires were sniffing the air." Tori said. She sits up putting her wine down to pace behind the couch. She is like a caged cat when she gets frustrated.

"I'm thinking with the changes that are happening with us hitting 25 our scent and signatures are changing. We may have to come up with a way to mask them." I try to make some logic out of this. My brain is on overload and just wants to shut down.

Looking at Chloe I can see the wheels turning. Knowing her, she may have a solution by morning. "Ok, here is what I am thinking. I can look into some herbals and oils that might help with the smell but I can't do anything about our signatures. I think that they were more interested in you than us." Chloe said, putting up her hand. "Let me finish. Tori, I need you to use your healing powers to get to the root of what is going on in her system. You have healed her before, maybe you can detect what is different about her." Tori finally stopped pacing. She tilted her head looking at me as a test subject.

I felt like a lab rat.

Holding her hands out in front of her she flexes her fingers and cracks them saying. "I can try, but my gift may not be able to see that because technically she isn't injured or sick." That is true, she is not an empath.

I try to relax as she looks into my eyes holding both sides of my head. I feel her warm energy over my cool skin. After a few minutes, she pulls back looking defeated. "I'm guessing you didn't find anything." Looking down at my wine to hide my disappointment. Watching her go back around to begin pacing again. "No, but yes you do feel different. I don't know why this is but your cells are different. Even your skin is cooler than normal. You said that your ice gift feels more settled within you. This may be why your signature has changed and what you smell of frost." Tori says. She braces her hands on the couch looking down at me. I look back up into her deep brown eyes that look black in this dim lighting. She looks a little scary when she is like this.

"Here is the thing, I think you should take on your full form for us. I want to see if you look different." Chloe asks, coming over sitting on the edge of the couch. She squeezes my knee keeping her hand on my leg. Closing my eyes, taking a deep breath, I say. "I think that is a good idea, I am just really overwhelmed so give me some space." I hand her the wine to walk around the couch.

There is more room between the kitchen and the living room than in the living room for this.

Tori moves to the stool at the counter to wait.

I take a couple of deep breaths clutching my hands in and out of a fist. I call on my wings that are tucked away. I take my shirt off to give them room and not destroy my sweater. Tori gives me a whistle from behind me, so I turn to throw my sweater at her. She just catches it waving it like a prize she won. She sure does know how to lighten the mood.

Ok, I rolled my shoulders calling them out. I stumble forward from the force at which they come out. Tori lunges forward catching me. Standing up, she and Chloe circle me. Taking a look, myself I can already see that my grey wings are tipped with white. I gasp at the sight of them. They are truly beautiful. "My color has changed. And I don't know if they are somehow stronger." I say. "You are right, they are different. Can you put them away now and show us what they look like in your aura?" Chloe asked. "Yeah, but I think they don't want to be put away," I state, pushing harder to put them back inside me.

After a few seconds, they finally listened to me. Panting, I look over my shoulder. Raising an eyebrow at them they finally walk around to the side and then to the front. "Ok, yep they are showing more and they are more intricate than before. They also are doing something to the skin on your back. I think you may need to take a look." Chloe says, touching my shoulder.

I race upstairs to my room skidding in front of my mirror. I turn around gasping at the intricate wings that look Celtic. Staring at my shoulders going down my back. I shift in the light as they are silver. They dim as I shift. When I shift again, they are more apparent. Strange but again beautiful.

I go back downstairs holding out my hand for my sweater. "That is new. I don't remember seeing anything like this on the other Valkyries. But I guess we were too young to notice." I sit back down grabbing my wine taking a big gulp. "We will figure this out. In the meantime, don't let anyone see your back." Tori says hugging me from the back over the couch. "Yeah, that is what I am thinking too. Thank you guys but we have more problems than this going on. What are we going to do about Kyro Industries and the vampires?" I get up walking back over to the fridge to refresh my wine.

Turning back to my friends I move on. "Look I'm glad we are figuring me out but I think we have two other pressing matters. One, I think we should still go after this experiment. I think it might be better in our hands than there's. We can do some research tomorrow to find out more about the company and then track down some of their other employees to get some answers. Second, in a little while, there will be some royals and our boss ringing that doorbell soon. What are we going to tell them?" I say take another careful breath.

Just as Chloe opens her mouth the buzz from the intercom starts up. Walking over to It Tori asks. "Who is it?" The response has my hair on the back of my neck standing up. "This is Lucas Storm, let us up." He says in that deep voice, making my toes curl.

Tori pushes the button to release the door for them to come up. I walk over to the couch with my wine trying to hide from view for a little bit to collect myself. Taking another sip of my wine I can feel my back tingling. I try to harness the ripple going under my skin. I push the ice to that part hoping to calm the area down. Slowly my back starts to feel normal-ish.

I hear the door open as they all pile into the apartment.

In a second, I am looking into the eyes of Lucas.

I spilled some wine on my sweatshirt. "Shit! Wear a bell or something!" I say pushing past him to go change my shirt. He grabs my arm stopping me from getting past him. He takes the wine away from me, handing it behind him to Eric. I try to pull away but he pushes me back onto the couch. "Umph" That was not nice. "No, you are not going anywhere till you explain what the hell is going on. I will personally have the damn sweater cleaned or replaced if that will get you to not try to get up and explain things." His deep voice comes out velvety smooth with a hint of a don't defy me heir to it.

Yeah, that voice alone will make my knees weak. I lean my head back taking another breath. Opening my eyes, I see him sitting on the coffee table in front caging me in with his legs. I sit up more trying to get some composure. "Fine, I'll do the best I can to tell you what is going on. Everyone might as well take a seat." Mason took my wine from Eric sitting on the hearth of the fireplace. "Mason, is it? Give me back my wine." Lucas turned to reach out; he took it, giving him a stern look of disapproval. Everyone else took a seat but Lucas remained right where he was. I took a large swallow of the wine letting it linger on my tongue. Looking at Ry I can see he was going to get impatient soon.

Patience can run low at this time of night.

"Where do you want me to start?" Tilting my head. Lucas leans forward saying. "Start with what you are and why your gifts are manifesting. Then, let's discuss your visions and how they pertain to me. Don't deny this because judging how your friend is about to interrupt me they do." With that, Tori leaned back glaring at him. I just let out a small smile. "Ok, for starters you don't need to know what I am. I have a couple of gifts but they are growing and developing." I try to be vague but let's face it, he just glared at me harder. "You know I can get this out of you eventually. Why don't you want us to know what you are? Ry can you tell me what they are?" He angled himself to put Ry into view. "I have asked the same question for years but I was never given a straight answer. I too would like to know girls. You can trust that we already know you are something different and special. Not many people can do the things you do. It is one of the reasons I invested in your business. I can see the souls of fighters in you." Ry says, taking a seat in the chair.

He knew how to twist the heart. "To tell you the truth it isn't that important. What is important is that yes, I think you are connected to the vision. I don't have an idea of how yet. I think it would be best if I showed you the vision from this morning that was replayed but the second time I was able to manipulate it." Reaching forward, I motion for him to lean in. "I will only let you into that part of my mind. You will not be able to go any further so don't even try to get access to the rest of me. I will project what is in my mind, to your mind. Are you ready?" He leans into my hands. I can feel him shudder under my touch. I am used to this because I am naturally cold compared to most people. Strangely, his skin doesn't have the normal human temperature but it is still a bit warmer than mine. Shaking this off I reach out to his mind making a bridge for him to enter. I feel the pressure of his mind pushing into mine. I block the need to hold him back. As he pushes through I hear a gasp as he sees what I have seen.

After a few minutes, I start to pull away but he snakes out his hands grasping my head pulling it in touching our heads. I feel him go deeper. Shit no! I push against him. Hearing the others getting up to defend me. I reach down for my ice, feeding it through my forehead into him. I hear a sharp intake before he releases me.

Falling back, I am out of breath and not happy.

I reach forward, punching him in the face. Seeing his head go back. Having that look of shock on his face, knowing a girl just got the upper hand was awesome. I took advantage of the shock. Pouncing on him I straddle his upper half on the coffee table. I channel the ice to my fingers creating a small knife. I hold it in place by his throat. "What the fuck?! I said not to go deeper. I showed you what you needed. Do not try that again." Waiting for the answer I look at my friends who are being detained by his brothers and Ry slowly comes forward like a mediator. "Ok, everyone calm down. Lucas, that was not a good way to build the trust we talked about." He said dryly.

Lucas just tilted his head, shrugging his shoulders. "Can't blame me for trying but I do have one question: what is so important about April 22nd at 9:40 am?" My turn to be shocked at what he was able to discover.

He played this to his advantage, knocking the knife out of my hand. He then put one arm around me flipping me on my back, holding my wrists securely in his grasp. "I want everyone to leave us. We have to discuss things further and all of you are getting in my way." He commanded. I flinch under his gaze. The weight of him not bugging me but the position was compromising.

Tori yells at him." Let her go, you asshole! There is no way we are leaving her alone with you." With an agreeing "Hell NO" from Chloe. I can see the plant in the corner starting to reach forward to defend her. Not wanting bloodshed, I thankfully hear a voice of reason. "I think that this is enough excitement for one night, Prince Lucas. I think any further discussions can be made tomorrow night. I do believe we should leave. These girls are not to be trifled with. They are very powerful." Ry interjects loudly with the voice of not just authority but with the air of a father. I can see his brothers waiting for his command. I for one am just plain worn out.

The hands and body above feel so good but the intent of him scares the living shit out of me. How can I be attracted to such a person as this? I clear my throat saying. "Please, just let me go. I will go downstairs with you to the VIP balcony and we can talk or we can talk here but your brothers need to go downstairs. My friends will go upstairs to their rooms and Ry you should go downstairs as well. I think we need to discuss things with just the two of us." I shift some under his weight trying to find some way to get out of this position.

Lucas slowly let's go of my wrists sitting back on the couch. I slowly prop myself up on my elbows. He offers out his hand to help me the rest of the way up. Thankfully there are no more visions tonight when I touch him. I need to get a handle on when and where I have them. Straightening up I look at everyone arguing with each other. Lucas stands up next to me putting his hand on the small of my back. Looking up into his face I can see the temper below the control. "I will agree with your friends being upstairs and everyone else down in the bar. I promise not to hurt you if that makes everyone feel better," he says. Tori throws up her hands walking to the stairs and Chloe points to her eyes with two fingers then back at him. In a telling sign off *I will be watching you* sign. I loved my friends.

Ry gave me one last look before hesitatingly walking to the door under the stairs. His brothers stayed. "I said for you to go down to the bar. I will be fine," he said to them. Mason stepped forward. "No, we need to know what she is and why we are connected just like you. Just because you are going to be king doesn't make us any less brother, just remember that." He says pointing his finger angrily at Lucas. Eric put his hand out on Mason's chest to stop him from going forward. "We will go downstairs, brother. We will discuss what will be said later. I do believe Lucas has the right to this for I can sense a connection between them." He states this by bowing and walking away. "Wait? What?... What do you mean by a connection?" I yell at his back as Mason and Eric walk over to the door. He looks over his shoulder saying. "Lucas, you better explain. We will meet you downstairs. He pushes Mason the rest of the way through the door. We are alone.

CHAPTER 9

Looking up into those eyes I could feel the pull. Had no idea that the pull to him meant we were connected. He puts pressure on my back to place me in front of him fully. I put my hands upon his chest out of defense pushing a tad. He looks down at me. "I think not my little imp. I think it is better to keep you in my grasp. It is less likely that you will have the room to punch me again." He is right, I would. Smirking, I say. "Fine, can we at least sit?" He looks behind himself to sit. I quickly bring my elbows down and out breaking his loose grip. I jump on the end of the couch with my blanket. I cover my lap up hugging the extra material at the top. I give him a look of *don't fuck with me.*

He shrugs his shoulders and sits near my feet that are up on the couch in front of me. He reaches taking my feet and legs across his lap resting his hands and lower arms on top. I try to pull them back in but let's face it at least I had the rest of me free.

I settle back down leaning into the turquoise pillow behind me. Looking at him this way he almost looks normal. Well, the fancy suit didn't fit with the situation but yep, he looked pretty relaxed. As if sensing this he reached up loosening his tie making it hang down in two strips on his upper chest. Then he unfastened the top two buttons. I quickly looked away feeling the need to reach out to help him.

Shifting my shoulders I ask. " What does it mean that we are connected? What would your brother know about this?" His gaze finds mine. "The reason he can tell is he is an empath. He can feel things and sense things that others cannot. The connection is harder to explain and I don't think you are ready to hear it. I think we will need to gain some trust before we can discuss this." Being told this, like I am a child that has no brain is more than insulting. "I don't think so, so I have enough to worry about. I need to know what this connection is about." I state like a sulking child. His low chuckle spoke of the fact he probably knew this. "Ok, I will tell you the truth about this if you answer my questions." Very sly move but effective.

I sigh nodding yes at him.

"Well let us start at the beginning. What are you?" He asked, running his hand up my leg. It felt so good I have never had a man do this before. Taking a breath, I hug the blanket at my waist a little tighter. "I am one of the few who can see the past and future. I also can go there as well to interact with it. Before today no one was able to see me in these visions and I was not able to interact with them. I don't know why this is linked to you. I still have not seen you in the vision. Both times it was the same people and the same setup. The only difference was that the second time, I needed to use my gift to protect them. I have never felt my ice gift pulling at me to use it before. Before today it wasn't fully settled in me but now it feels 99% settled. But I have a feeling that you do." I say pointedly to him before continuing. "Now your turn. How are you connected to my vision and me?" He moves his hand to my thigh pulling me deeper down into the couch. I feel my sweatshirt slide up some from being moved. His wicked grin matched the mischief in his eyes. I try not to swallow my tongue at the sexy vampire holding my legs hostage.

Looking away from him I slow my breathing down before looking back at him. He is thinking of something. The way his eyes travel over me, I feel like a lab rat again. Just like when Tori did this earlier but with him, I felt the danger in his assessment. "What you just told me is not what you are but of the gifts that you possess. I know that some species come into their gifts later in life and a few of them have gifts that continue to develop throughout their lives. I get the feeling that you are in either of these groups. So again what are you?" This guy is like a dog with a bone. He wasn't letting this go easily.

Rolling my shoulders back I try to sit up a little bit more but he applies slightly more pressure to my legs holding me in place. Fine I guess I am going to stay put. "I am not going to tell you my species because it is too dangerous for you to know." I try to get the dangerous part across but I have the feeling that this will not deter him.

"You want to know something; we vampires have heightened senses. For example, the race of your pulse is calling to me and your breathing has changed ever so slightly. Especially when I move my hand up." His hand moves up proving his point.

I slap my hand on top of his hand causing him to stop moving up. He chuckles at me before going on. "I guess I should play nice with my future mate, but I for one am wanting to push those buttons because your eyes darken like the forest at night. I will stop asking for now what you are but eventually, you will tell me." Hearing the word mate has me in panic causing me to skip right over the cockiness of the fact he says that I will eventually tell him what I am.

Stuttering as I try to get it all out. "What do you mean by mate? You are a vampire; we cannot possibly be mates. It has been 100's of years since a vampire has mated outside its species and it was very hard the last time this happened for the person being changed." Hearing myself say this doesn't negate the pull I feel for him.

I can feel my breathing getting dangerously fast. Last time I had a panic attack I passed out. I sit forward, dragging in the air trying to calm down. Lucas leans in taking my forehead against his again but instead of trying to push his way in he spoke to me. "Ok take it easy, we need to calm that breathing down. No need to hyperventilate. Breath with me, you can do this." I start to match his breathing as he first matches mine before bringing his breathing down to a normal level.

After getting my breathing back he kisses my forehead saying. "That's a good girl." I slowly pull back from him. I can't believe what is happening. This is not possible. Ok, I try to focus on the fact that I had an answer, but it was hard, it can't be true right? After a few more breaths with him just letting me process this I can form a sentence. "I am not saying I believe you but how is this connection related to the visions. You saw the same demons that I did. I mean even the skeleton tattoo guy said to "get her". I was the only girl on that pier."

Hugging the blanket to my abdomen helps.

His hands are distracting as all hell. They keep stroking and moving effortlessly on my legs.

He leans his head back on the couch with a sigh. "To think I was warned of a potential mate but I never figured we would meet under these circumstances. Ok, yes the man did say this, and I will find out what this has to do with you for I don't think he is done. From my other dealings, I have seen these demons before and they are not just hired one at a time. I found more this morning deeper in the woods. I have an idea they were there for you. Putting your vision and this morning together paints that picture. My only hold up is why your vision took you to the past both times to the exact moment and the second time you were able to interact with it and change the outcome." Lucas blows out an exasperated breath at his explanation. He gets up and starts pacing. I tuck my legs under myself shifting to look up at him.

After a few minutes of this, I finally came to an answer. "I think that vision was a teachable one. Look at it this way there is no real way to practice my vision gift like you would with fire. With fire you create. It is physically there. With a vision, it's all about the mind... No, hear me out. I have a gift that was passed to me and after the first time, I felt compelled to use this gift more than my others. I don't usually use it for the fact that it has never fully settled in me. The thing is after I had the second vision, I used the gift to not only change what had happened to those Vikings but it settled inside me like it was finally finding its home. I have no idea why the skeleton tattoo guy was there but I fought him off and solidified my gift to myself. For all we know, they could have been drawn to me through the vision, in control or I was interrupting the regular time and they were always supposed to be there." Saying this all out loud in front of a stranger was weird for me. I never did this outside of Tori and Chloe.

He had stopped pacing a few feet away from me. Looking up at him I can see the wheels turning in his head. "This may be my gift trying to settle itself inside me by connecting with one of my other gifts, I was going to go do some research tomorrow to figure this out and I have some friends that I can consult with. So let's move on to the fact that you found more of those demons in the woods." I cock one eyebrow up at him as I say this.

He shook his head at me looking up at the ceiling. "Wait, where do you plan on researching and who are you going to talk to? You cannot tell anyone about us as of yet for we need to first move you to my estate for your protection. Don't give me that baffled look you know how there was an attack on the royal court at Sky restaurant. People are trying to take over and they will kill for it. And those demons with their master could have been there for the simple reason to kidnap you. You were fading into the vision. I am guessing your gift is developing so that you can go to the past or future." Hearing him say all this puts me on edge and hicks up my angry side. Pushing back from the couch I stand up to face him. "Look you may be my mate or whatever this is going on between us but you don't get to demand things from me. You got it?" I say turning my back on him I walk around the couch to the sink to get some water.

Thinking back to the vision and the fact that he had to call me out of it was scary. I could also feel him when I was there but it was very faint. I think he is right about my vision gift developing in this way but I think that I was also there to learn about my other gift. Doing this with him may be part of the mate thing. Maybe my soul recognizes him and thinks this is a good time to evolve. Shrugging to myself I turn to face Lucas.

I wish my mind would calm down.

All of this cannot be happening. I just can't be his mate. I am a Valkyrie. We are fierce warriors. I am reciting this to myself as I drink an entire glass of water. Watching him cross over to where I am in the kitchen almost makes me want to either punch him or jump his bones.

He then moved right behind me leaning on the island countertop. His arms are across his chest making his muscles look even bigger. We stare at each other for a few seconds before he says anything. "I am used to giving orders. I am the crown prince and you will have to come to terms with this. Now for those demons in the woods, yes we did find more but some got away. I was not the only one in the area that day searching for these demons. My guards and I were alerted to them by one of our people in the Patrol office. These demons are linked to some thefts, around not just our town but other cities as well and they all seem to wear this pendant on a leather strap." Putting my hands up to stop him I race away from him shouting over my shoulder. "Hold on, I found the same on the demon that I killed." I race up the stairs blowing past Chloe and Tori who are eavesdropping. I find the pullover in the washing machine getting the forgotten necklace out of the pocket. I ran back downstairs with the girls this time following me. Holding up the pendant so we can see that the pendant has a skull on it. "Do the other necklaces have a skull pendant on them?" Judging by his face that is true. He gives me a curt nod.

Turning to my friends, I can see that they are not only shocked but are going to go kill someone if we don't come up with a play. Thinking fast, I turn back to Lucas. "There is a lot for us to talk about but I think we should do some more research on this symbol and how it is connected to those demons. We can access the private section of the library. The three of us are going there tomorrow to do some research on another aspect of our business. We can check out the books and archives for this as well." Judging by his face he is not sold on this.

I turn to walk back to where Tori and Chloe are standing at the end of the island. I feel a tug on my sweater pulling me back into a hard chest. Gasping at the connection of his full body pressed up against my back. I automatically cover the hand on my stomach. Feeling his breath in my ear. I put my other hand up signaling for my friends not to interfere. "I think we are not done talking little imp. But I will let you go for now. I have connections that will be researching this. Tomorrow night we can meet up to discuss what we have found. I have more questions and you still haven't answered what you are." He says this in a low voice that is so enticing. I turn my head up replying. "Fine, can we meet here again? Also, is Mason going to be a problem? He doesn't seem to be as in-control as you are." I can feel him stiffen at this last part.

With his grip on my waist loosened some, I can turn around to look into his face. His gaze finds mine immediately. The red ring around the eyes is back and I push against his chest to get some distance from those fangs. "I do believe that tomorrow it would be best if you came to my estate. I have resources there that are going to be useful and the security is better. As for my brother, yes he is in control. Just when he is already compromised it slips. I will make sure this never happens around you and your friends. For you are the most appealing creature to me. I will send a car to pick you and your friends up at 5." Lucas says all of this with the authority of his title.

It will be interesting to see this estate and to see what resources he has. We are good at getting the information that we need legally and illegally. We all learned to hack at an early age. It has come in handy, not just with our business but with how we can hide our identities from the world. "Ok, then I'll see you tomorrow night." Why did it feel wrong to be saying goodbye?

Shit, this man has been grabby, forceful, and intrusive to me since we met.

To top that all off, he is a vampire.

CHAPTER 10

Rolling over to reach for the damn phone that was beeping was pure torture. I finally managed to grab it. Cracking my eyes open I see that it is from Ellie.

Even her texts were too chipper for their own good, at this hour. Which is, shit 10:35 am! I had to get my ass moving if we were going to get the intel we needed on Kyro Industries and the royals.

Rolling over onto my back, I text back. *Sorry just getting up. Where did you want to have coffee? I can be out the door in 10 minutes.* Pushing myself fully up I try to remember what was all said last night. I just get the feeling that I don't have enough information.

Rubbing my chest, I feel an ache like something is missing.

Getting up still rubbing my chest I look into my closet seeing some comfy stretchy jeggings that will go with the black blouse. Tugging them on running them up my legs reminds me of the hands that had played with them last night. Stopping myself from moaning out loud, I shift to get the black boots and leather jacket.

Rushing to the door I hear the shower on and a really bad ballad being sung from the shower. Yikes, yep that has to be Tori for she can't sing worth crap. Neither can I, but man at least we usually keep our voices from leaving the apartment. Rushing into the bathroom for my morning rituals yelling over the music to Tori. "Hey, I'll meet you guys at the library. I am going to have coffee with Ellie and ask her about the Vikings in my vision." She stuck her head out around the shower curtain saying. "Sure, that sounds good. I think Chloe already has been playing on the computer this morning. I'll go talk with her after my shower. Cya later." She pops her head back in to sing so the radio some more.

If I had time, I would dump a glass of cold water on her. Leaving the diva to her music, I ran to Chloe's room finding it empty. Going downstairs I find her on the couch with her laptop, hacking away. Smiling, I come up behind her hugging her over the top of the couch.

I look over her shoulder at the document that I am sure is from Kyro Industries. Reading some of the print I can see that this company is into experiments, big time. "Where did you find this? How far back in their history have you gone so far?" I ask her, resting my chin on her shoulder. She replies without looking away from the screen. She must be on a roll for this to happen. "I hacked into their main server under a worm I was able to follow. I have gone through a few years so far but believe me when I say this, they are not doing these experiments for the greater good. In these reports, there are detailed notes about some of their experiments not just exploding but escaping. They are doing these experiments on test subjects that I think aren't willing." This takes me back a few steps from her.

Staring at the wall in shock I keep thinking that we almost made a deal to do a job for them. This could blow up at any moment. If the public knew about these experiments, I wonder what would happen to them. I for one know that you can't do all this without supporters and what if it is our government helping them.

I didn't have time to sit and listen to the rest because I received a text from Ellie.

That's ok I handed in my paper a little late, so I had to sweet talk to the professor not to do it for it. I am on my way to the bar to help with some inventory so I will just meet you downstairs in about 5 minutes.

Thank my lucky stars! "Hey, I will be downstairs when you are ready to go to the library having coffee with Ellie. She may have some answers about the Vikings in my vision." Throwing my jacket on, I head for the door to go downstairs.

Chloe absently waves at me from the couch saying "Sure thing, yeah" haha she is not going to remember so I shout the same thing upstairs to Tori who gives me a more all-together answer. "Yeah, can you push the button on the coffee machine on your way out?" I shout back to her, turning to push the button. "Yep, your diesel is brewing!"

Walking down to the bar I had a weird feeling. Cracking the door at the bottom of the steps I can see the back of a black jacket on a tall frame. As he turns his head I can tell that he is not human. I do the only logical thing I know and that is pushing the door all the way open into the guy causing him to stumble forward. I immediately go for a punch to the face but he blocks my fist. Going low he came back up reaching for me. He gets a hold of my arm. As I try to kick him, he locks that leg under the arm. "Look I am not here to hurt you. Please stop trying to punch me or you will hurt yourself. I was ordered by the crown prince to guard you and your friends." He explained, all the while I was trying to catch my breath.

He dropped my leg and let go of my arm when I nodded my head. Looking him up and down I can see he is one lethal dude. There is a wicked-looking blade hanging from his leather belt. That is secured to a long frame of pure muscle and stealth. His square jaw with the dimple did nothing to hide the glint of a killer. His eyes had the red ring around the grey that showed I had come close to bringing the beast out of him.

Stepping back, I tilt my head to one side trying to figure out if I should be pissed or not. "I can tell now that you are a vampire, but seriously you could have told us one of you is down here." My glare did nothing to get this man to back up, even a little. Moving to go around his arm shoots out, stopping me from proceeding. Looking up into those eyes again. "I need you to wait for the rest of my team to get here before one of you tries to leave. I can't guard you all if you aren't in the same place." He simply states. Wow, this guy needed to back off. "Look, I am going downstairs to have coffee with a friend. When we leave, my friends will more than likely pull the car around to pick me up. So let me by or we are going to have an issue." Crossing my arms leaning on my right leg, I give him my glare of death.

Looking down at his phone I can see him checking for any messages. I roll my eyes at him and walk to the balcony. I guess that was aloud.

He quickly scrolls through his contacts finding the one he wants finally. As he is talking into the phone I take a look at the ledge. Yep, I can get there and jump down before he can get to me. Taking one last look, I rush over to the ledge, jumping up and calling out to Ellie down below. I feel my feet leave the ledge but all of a sudden, I am being grabbed by the waist, hauled back up over the ledge. "Holy shit woman! Are you trying to kill yourself?" This guy had no idea who he was dealing with. "No, I am not. I can jump down from here and land like I am walking through the park. So let me go, vamp." Just then I hear Ellie yelling from downstairs at someone else that I think just came into the bar.

Looking over the ledge, still, in the vampire's hold, I realize it is Eric and Mason. Well shit, this just got more interesting by the second. Turning up to the vampire holding me I say. "That's the team you are waiting for. Well fine, can I go down now?" He is still looking at me when he sniffs the top of my head. His hand moves up my abdomen turning me around. I look into the blood-red eye that used to be grey. Shit, this is not good. All of a sudden Eric is on the ledge in the back of me. "Let her go, Simon. I can understand your pull to her but she is not for you." Eric reaches out his hand, loosening Simon's hold on me.

I stagger back into the arms of Eric who whispers in my ear. "I think it best if you get your friends. We need to talk." Thinking to myself *yeah, no shit*. I turn around to Eric still hearing Ellie down below berating Mason. She is going to get herself in trouble, where the hell is Ace. I walk over to the ledge again but put my finger up to stop the two vampires behind me. Yelling down to Ellie. "Ellie, hey! These are the special guests from last night. Trust me they are fine but I think that you should go back to do your inventory so we can have a coffee at a different time." I try to give her a reassuring face but I am not doing a good job. "Fine, but you holler if these guys give you any trouble and I'll send my muscle out." She yells back, giving me a wave as she walks over to go through the doors to the kitchen.

Seeing her out of the way from harm I finally focus on Mason downstairs. He is casually dressed in black pants and a red shirt with a leather jacket over the top, but the difference in his appearance is the eyes. They were more relaxed today. Not an ounce of red around the eyes and his skin appeared to be less shiny. Turning back to Eric I see him giving the guy he called Simon some new orders.

He walks back over to me shaking his head. "You were supposed to sleep longer. We didn't anticipate you being up this early. I also heard you will be leaving soon for the library. I think it is best if we come with you. Some things have developed while you have been sleeping, Lucas fears that you are not safe. We can talk about this more tonight, away from prying ears." He motions for me to come with him. I see no point in not doing this so I follow him over to our door in the alcove. I rest my hand on the door letting it feel me out. I hear the pop of the lock. I open it with Eric and Mason following me up the stairs, with Simon at his guard station once again.

Opening the door at the top of the stairs I shout out. "Guys, we have some company!" Tori looks up from her breakfast burrito and Chloe tries to turn around on the couch to see who was there. Moving aside I let them see the two vampires entering our apartment.

Leaning against the wall by the door, seeing their reactions were just right. Though I think Tori may need to close her mouth. I open mine then use my hand to close it. Nodding my head to her. She took the hint, closing her mouth not so gracefully. "So I didn't make it down to the bar but I think that these guys can explain that a little more than I can. Chloe, can you grab the shades while I call down to Ellie, so she doesn't call the Patrol."

Vampires aren't incinerated by the sun but it does bug them. They usually stick to the nighttime, which does nothing to fix the stereotype for some people.

A quick call down proves that she was about to do just that but after I had her talk to us on speaker, she was more apt to let this go. She agrees to meet later this week if I still have questions about the Vikings.

Walking over to the counter I stand next to Chloe and Tori waiting for the explanation of why we aren't safe. Clearing my throat I get this little party started. "Ok, what is going on? Why aren't we safe?" I demand.

Mason moves forward, angling himself to be more in front. He rolls his eyes, shaking his head at my demands. "The details are not important for you to know right now. This will all be explained later when you come to the estate. Just do what you are told human and be happy you are under our protection at this moment." He states with some flair of his hand that is resting on the counter.

Wow, was this asshole seriously trying to be in charge. He is the one who got high last night and couldn't control himself and now he is looking down on us as lowly humans. If only we could tell them that we are Valkyries. That would take him down a few pegs.

Eric put his hand on his brother's shoulder pushing him against the wall before we could respond. "You are not to be giving any orders. You are on thin ice as it is. Your little speech was callous and not one to be given. Shut your mouth, before I shut it for you." His voice is so calm it is scary. I only know of one person who can do that and that is Chloe. I thought she was scary but with the red eyes and fangs showing, he may have her beat.

He turned to us with some red still on the edge of his eyes but the fangs had retracted, thank the Gods for that. Mason stays by the wall with a full sulk going on. His face shows the hatred that he has at that moment for his brother.

Seeing this, I am tempted to rip his head off. No idea why but it would feel good.

Eric proceeds back to the kitchen island, stopping at the same spot his brother had once stood. Lowering his head is a small bow he says. "I am sorry for my brother. He is still learning how to deal with other species and how to control that smart mouth of his." After a beat, he continues. "We are here to help at the library, to find more information about the vision. We also heard that a company is more than a little peeved at you right now for not doing a job, on their terms. Between the mate connection with Lucas and this company we think it wise to have us around for protection till we can figure this all out." Hearing all this from him was odd and comforting at the same time but with him being an empath he could be trying to control the way we feel.

Chloe stood up from her chair, walking around to Eric. "Thanks for the apology but we do not need or want your protection. We are good on our own. The company you are referring to is not a big threat. We can handle them." She is definitely in her *take no to shit* mode. Normally, I would agree with her but I think keeping them close might be beneficial to see what they are also digging up.

Looking to Tori, who is still giving Mason the stink eye, I take over. "Eric normally I agree with Chloe but I think it won't hurt to have more people searching for the information on this vision I had. Though she is right, we are good on our own with handling Kyro Industries. Let's form a truce for now. Ok?" Looking at Chloe and Eric I can see them sizing each other up. Tori leaned forward pointing at Mason. "This truce only works if certain people can control their over-inflated heads. You think you can keep your brother in line?" She says facing Eric. Mason pushes off the wall trying to protest this but Eric holds his arm out stopping him. "Yes, you have my word. He will respect the truce and if we are going to do this then everything you find will be for us as well. This vision has something to do with Lucas. Therefore, the court needs to follow through." I can live with this but there is no way we are going to be sharing anything to do with

Kyro Industries with them. Kyro Industries may have a problem with us not accepting their terms but we are still interested in the experiment that was stolen from them.

Chloe looks back at us for the nod before she reaches out to shake on it. After this she says. "This has to go both ways so no hiding information from us either. Now, what aren't you telling us and why?" She is always one to go the extra mile. Eric shifts like he is uncomfortable. Rolling his shoulders back before answering. "We don't have all the information to share yet but believe me, tonight we will have enough to tell you. If you are still going to the library then we should get going." He looks down at his watch then moves to the door.

Seeing as we were already going there, I moved to go with him. Tori stood up with her plate. "Alex, you go on ahead Chloe and I have some more research to do here. We can meet you back here in a few hours since you have them to help you look. We will continue on our end here." She says putting her plate into the sink. She turns around leaning up against the sink waiting for me to answer. Tilting my head side to side, I can see her point. "Yeah, that sounds good but give me a call if you need me back sooner." Giving them a wave, I turn to the door.

Eric holds it open for me and Mason who quickly follows without saying a word. Just before he walks through, he turns to say. "One of our guards will be at the base of the stairs for your protection. If you need to leave, have him go with you but I advise you to stay here." The door swings shut without us hearing their reply.

Descending the stairs, I can't help but have my guard up. With two vampires behind me and one that has been proving to be a loose cannon. Getting to the bottom I open the door to Simon who looks pissed as fuck. "Ok big guy what has your feathers ruffled?" saying stepping to the other side for Eric and Mason to get through. Simon glares at me and then puts his attention on Eric. "You need to go downstairs and deal with her friends. They are threatening to call the Patrol and they seem to not be able to get a hold of Mr. Riley to confirm that we can be here."

After he stated this, he seemed to relax just getting this all out. Must be one of those now it is your problem, not mine anymore. Eric reached for his phone and Mason whispered under his breath. "Damn Humans!" These guys had to work on their social skills. Most of us are beyond human. That may be our base but really not our species. "I will go down to talk to my friends and I will leave a message with Ry on why you are here guarding my door. Does this work for everyone?" Looking at them I then just turn walking to the stairs. Not even bothering to wait for the reply.

I see that Brian is back. Waving at him to come forward I met him at the door. "Hi, so there are some vampires here. If you remember Prince Eric and Prince Mason." I motioned to them as they staggered behind me. "They're leaving one of their guards up by our door in case Tori and Chloe need anything. They promise not to cause any problems while they are here and I will tell Ry all about this I promise." Looking up into Brian's face I can see the questions flash in his eyes. I shake my head slightly to indicate he shouldn't ask. A frown forms on his face sending me his big brother's protective face. "I don't agree with this but if you vouch for them, then I will not call the Patrol. Make sure you talk to Ry. Be careful or I will be forced to avenge you." Smiling, I reach up and kiss him on the cheek. "Don't worry, I got this! I'll see you later." He hugs me before he lets me go. Watching us walk out the door. As we reach the pavement Eric turns me around by the shoulder. "What were you doing kissing that man? Is he your boyfriend?" He is looking down at my face level, with Mason right behind him trying to pull him back. "I kissed my friend on the cheek because I wanted to and no he is not my boyfriend. Can you let go of me now?" Saying this was weird. I know there is a possible mate connection between me and Lucas but what does that have to do with Brian or who I choose to date.

Eric shakes his brother off while letting go of me. He walks a few paces to an SUV parked at the curb. Mason pushes me forward to the SUV while Eric holds open the door to the back for me. Sliding into the plush black leather seat I realize how dark it is inside the vehicle. Trying to adjust my eyes, I blink a few times. Leaning back into the seat I wait for them to load in so to speak. Mason swings into the front passenger seat and Eric slides in next to me.

Eric reaches across me, taking the buckle himself. After this, he sits back telling the driver to go. The shock wears off soon after for me to ask again. "What is going on? You didn't answer my question." Turning to him. Rubbing his hand over his face he drops it to his lap facing me. "You are right I didn't answer your question, for it is not mine to answer. After tonight you will be able to get those questions answered. Can you please wait till then? I promise this will all make more sense after." Weighing my options in my head I can see Mason glancing in the rearview mirror. His smirk is one I want to smack off his face.

Turning my attention back to Eric I say. "Yes, but if they are not answered I will kick your ass." With a small smile, Eric says. "I accept this, but don't you think you will be in over your head?" Haha yeah, but like hell, I am going to admit that to him. I shrug my shoulders, looking out the window the rest of the way to the library.

CHAPTER 11

Getting into the library with them was easy but the way they stayed in the shadows freaked me out. I need to pick up a book on vampires. Before this, we never needed to look them up. Simply for the fact that vampires stay on their side of town. They also have their own government to handle most of their problems without needing to use the city's government. At least that is what we know; this is true of the Fae also.

The Fae and Vampires are races that keep to themselves. There is some literature on them but even that is limited. I have been told that there are libraries in each of these communities but I don't know where they are in them. To get access to these libraries you have to go through their courts. Each court has a king and council that control their part of town. The misfit or the other species adhere to the rules set by the overall government. Which is weird. No idea why there is such a divide between these two species and the rest of us.

On entering the back library the two vampires quickly shut all the large curtains blocking out the light. Sighing, I walk over to the section on Vikings and start to pick up a few books on their history and why this culture is a part of the supernatural world. There aren't many of them. They must seamlessly put themselves into our world for them to just become part of the fabric of our community.

I begin to page through the book on the top of my stash. There is some information about the culture of the non-gifted versus the gifted. The main gift these people tended to have was of the sea and more point-edly, on how they were able to control it. There, of course, are some with other gifts but those were not in as great of detail but there were references for other areas to look at for details on these people that were later writ-ten in. Seeing that Mason looked not busy leaning against the bookshelf nearby I called out to him. "Since you said you are here to help, how about pulling these books marked in this book while I go through the next book on my stack." Holding the book out to him, seeing the sneer across his face.

This guy had some issues when it came to other people he classes below himself. "I don't take orders from you!" He growls out at me. "No you don't, if you had listened; I asked you to do this, not demanded. But if you just want to stand there and be useless... then, by all means, continue," I state putting the book down I turn to the next one in the pile.

Eric steps around me on the floor picking up the book. I watch out of the corner of my eye as he approaches Mason. Smiling down at my book in my lap I try to make it look like I am engrossed in what I am reading.

Eric approached Mason holding out the book as I did. "So you need an order to get your ass moving to help, then fine. Do as she says and look for the books that are marked in here. I for one am not amused by your antics anymore today, so start helping or you will answer to Lucas for your actions. Just also remember I am his second, so I don't even have to take this to him. Furthermore, she is his mate. Making her the same level as Lucas. Don't forget this." Eric says this just low enough that I almost missed it. I see the intense posture of both of them leading to a fight so I decide to intervene. "Guys these books are not just old but one-of-a-kind in some ways, so don't start a fight here." Mason grabs the book from his brother walking away not saying a word. Eric turns back to me to say. "Yes, they are rare, how may I help now that Mason has been given his task." Looking up from my lap I can see he means it but behind all of this, I can sense him studying me.

Rolling my shoulders back, I position my back more against the bookshelf. "If you could take a look at one of the books Mason comes back with that would be great or start on one of the other books that I have pulled from the shelf that would be a good start."

After a few hours of us continuing to read and fetch more books I start to see a pattern. Not only did these books talk about the culture but how they survived. One of the many things mentioned in survival was the pillaging and conquering of villages. Sometimes they even took people and treasures from that village. I am guessing they have taken some rare and valuable things, making enemies in the process. "Ok, guys I think that I know what we need to do. I need to go back again to see what they were loading on that ship. A lot of what they did was not just sailing but pillaging other villages of other cultures. They would take not just valuables but also people. Usually in the female variety. I wonder what was in those crates that they took and why they were ok with leaving some behind." I say slowly trying to unfold myself from the floor.

OMG, my legs are so cramped! Why in the world didn't we move this to the couches and chairs? Using the bookshelf behind me I hoist myself off the ground to lean against the shelf.

Eric looks over to Mason who has just come back with another book that was referenced in the book on Eric's lap. "You want to go back to that vision but last time you almost went there fully. It was hard to pull you back out. I was watching you and Lucas together and I could see this energy passing between the two of you. I think he was anchoring you. Without him, you could have gone back in time. I already went through this with Lucas but I think it will be beneficial to you as well." Eric stood up opposite me leaning on the shelf. Mason stands with his arms crossed with the book in his hand in an aggressive stance. "I think we should stop and ask Lucas first what we should share with this human. We don't know if we can trust her." He states angrily.

Eric holds up his hand motioning for him to back off. "This information she can find for herself and judging by her resources she will soon." He says turning back to me. I just shrug my shoulders, smirking at him, for he is right. "The connection that has started between you and Lucas is rare and will grow over time. The fact that your gifts have started to develop after meeting him is a sign that the more you are around him the greater your powers will become. The strength you can pull from Lucas through the connection is causing your powers to grow. This is what my research has said so far." Eric leans forward gauging my reactions

This was a lot to take in for sure but I had no time to have a freak-out so I tried some of Tori's yoga breathing. After a few breaths, I opened my eyes seeing both of the vampires staring at me with perplexed looks on their faces. "If you are right about this then I think it is safe to say we are done here for now. I need to get back to my place to talk to my friends and eat." Taking this all in I start to pick up some of the books to put back when Eric motions with his hand sending all the books back to the shelves around the big room. Yep, that was cool no doubt about that. "Ok, umm thanks," I say following them to the door.

Walking out into the afternoon sun, I look at the two vampires putting on sunglasses that are more than just a normal tint judging by the black of the lens. Seeing how their faces get tenser I see that the sun affects them. Mason walks quickly to the SUV hopping into the front passenger seat. Eric opens the door for me once again motioning for me to get in.

I almost get to the door when I hear my name behind me. "Alex! I think we need to have another chat." I hear this from behind me so I turn to find the greasy ball Julian Gartor standing two feet behind me. Sizing him up I step forward. "What would we have to talk about? I think we made our viewpoints clear last night." I know now my smart mouth should have a little more sense not to use sarcasm but when a bastard just sets himself up like that, I have no choice.

Calling the ice to my hand envisioning a dagger. Tapping the formed dagger against my leg I waited for this idiot to try something. Hearing him clear his throat, four large men appear out of the SUV behind him. "I believe that we will have better luck with you coming with us to speak further." Julian is a little too cocky for his own good. I feel Eric come up behind me and hear Mason and the driver get out to stand behind Eric. I think my backup may be more than these bastards can handle. "Look, we agreed last night that your terms are not to our liking and that we are not taking this job. You think that you and your men can force me to come with you, then I would like you to meet my new friends." I say gesturing to the three vampires behind me.

Seeing Julian step back I think that I have won this round. "As I said, we need to talk to your friends. I believe they have retained some sensitive information that doesn't belong to them. I suggest that you and your friends return it and back off before someone gets hurt." Julian says.

Mason steps forward with Eric. In a flash, Eric has him by the front of his shirt and Mason clunks two of the others together causing them to become unconscious. "I think not, she is coming with us and under the protection of the vampire court from here on out. If you have a problem with her and her friends, make your concerns known to the court from now on. This is your only warning on this matter. I suggest that you pick your men up and leave the lady alone," said Eric. Dropping him back to his feet Julian motions for the other two guys to pick up their friends. He turns to leave but before he ducks into his vehicle he says. "This is not over."

Eric and Mason turn to me. I am surely expecting some answers but frankly, I had none until I spoke with my friends. "I don't know anything until I speak to my friends," I state, turning to go back to the SUV. I feel a small woosh of air and then I see that the door is held open again and Mason is already in the car.

Rolling my eyes to the heavens, I just think that was overkill. I mean I obviously can't move that fast so they will still have to wait for me to catch up. Sliding in again, I am amazed at the luxury of the vehicle. I am sure if I asked, there would be a bottle of champagne chilling with real crystal glasses in a hidden compartment.

I also wanted to play with all the buttons but I knew this would be a true sign of my innocence. I decided to clamp my hands together on my lap and pray that they follow what my brain says. I lean my head back, breathing in and thinking of not just the vision but the experiment. How did those guys know where to find me?

Unfortunately, my quiet time was not to last. "I just took out two guys for this human and I want to know why this is," Mason states over his shoulder at his brother. "This human is not going to talk to the bloodsucker in the front seat until he gets it through his thick skull, that being an asshole is not going to get anything from me." Opening my eyes, I then turn to Eric. "I don't know anything yet for I need to get home to talk to Chloe and Tori, they were researching them when we left." Leaning back again I reach out to open the window for some air. With my finger on the button, I feel a hand grab my wrist. "Please don't do that. If you need some more air then I will adjust the air back here." He says reaching up to the buttons on the ceiling conceal. I give up on opening the window. "After we get back, I think it would be wise not to leave till we come back at 5 o'clock. Simon will stay to keep guard but we have to return to the estate to prepare for tonight. After you have spoken to your friends, I think it would be wise for you to drop what you are doing that involves that company. They are dangerous people and I am warning you against going any further down whatever road that you are going." Hearing this from Eric only peaks my interest further in the pursuit. I am one stubborn woman and I hate it when someone says I can't do something.

Smiling at him I can't help but laugh at his last warning. "You realize that I am a grown woman with free will and I am choosing to go forward with this. They are doing things that I think are illegal and downright dangerous. Yes, I know some of this from my research. They may be dangerous but I can handle myself." We are pulling up in front of the Apothecary bar when Eric's phone goes off. He holds up a finger to me but I am not going to stick around to find out what it is. I open the door but Eric's hand shoots out grabbing my wrist again tugging me back into the SUV. "What the hell!" I yell at him.

Before Mason can say anything, Eric hangs up the phone. "That was Lucas. I think it best if you come with us to the estate instead of going upstairs." He motions for the driver to keep going. "What! No! Why would I come with you? What did he say on the phone?" I say in exasperation.

I reach for the second time and reach for the door but find that it is locked up and that no matter how many times I push the unlock button it simply won't open for me.

At this, my panic starts to set in. I lift the ice dagger that I quickly formed in my hand pointing it at Eric. "Tell me what is going on or I will use this." This time when he tries to use his speed against me I can anticipate this and duck the knife in time but he can recuperate quickly grabbing my hand with the dagger he then twists my arm making me turn my body into him holding me in a bear hold.

He talks to me calmly into my left ear. "I think it best if we wait till we get to the estate. All I was told was that it isn't safe for you to go up there. We will all find out together, then we get to the estate. Please stop trying to get out of the vehicle or I will hold you the rest of the way to the estate. I find this not to be a hardship to hold you. You do smell very appetizing." He smells my neck after saying this. This gets my heart rate up another few notches closer to that panic attack. Trying to contain my breathing I say. "Fine, I will behave. Let go of me." I feel the hold loosen slightly but then he asks. "Let me have that dagger first." Sighing, I slowly let the dagger drop from my hand into his. After he has it the hold is released on me.

Getting back to my side of the SUV I try to think of the reasons why I would not be allowed to return to my home. The only one I can think of is not good. Picking up my bag I get my phone out to contact one of my friends. Yet Eric voices out. "I think it best that you try not to contact anyone till we get there." The way he says this puts a chill going up my back.

I think he would take my phone if I tried to call anyone. I glare at him before putting my phone back into my bag. Mason then decides that this is the time to make another smart-ass comment. "Look at that, the human can learn. What a good girl you are." As he is cooing this at me, I make a small ice spear in my hand. Raising my hand like I am going to flick him off but instead, I aim for his hand that is on the center console. "Oww! Shit, what the fuck!" Hearing his howl of pain was very satisfying but crap I did just piss off a vampire. Mason pulls up the little ice spear from his hand and lungs for the back of the SUV. Eric intervenes, pushing him back into his seat telling him to *knock it off; he* deserved it for the smart comments.

Personally, I think he deserved it for being a jackass.

After Eric calmed his brother down, he came back to me. "Stop with the knives already, we will not hurt you and from now on Mason will refrain from the smart-ass comments. Is this something you can live with for now?" He is breathing heavily after getting this out and dealing with his brother. Shrugging at him I say "Yes, but if he continues, I will make more knives." This seems to satisfy him for he leans back in his seat running his hands down his face. The rest of the trip was quick and uneventful until we got closer to the vampire side of town.

The sun immediately was lost behind some clouds that I think are magically created to keep the sun out of this part of town. The gothic architecture is hauntingly beautiful in this light or should I say no light. Without the sun above us, everything seems to be in the shadows. I have only been here a few times but every time I come here I make sure it is short and without disturbing them.

Looking at the shops give way to houses and then to larger estates I have to think that this is where a lot of power is in this town. Not many in my part of town have this type of home or grandeur. As we near the mountain I see that a road goes up to a freaking castle.

That's what they call an estate; what the hell do they call a mausoleum. I know my mouth is hanging open but I simply can't seem to stop staring at this place as we get closer to the castle. I see that it is attached to the side of the mountain.

Going through the front gate of the place I see that it is not lacking in security. Not only are there cameras but also guards and some kind of hell beast walking the perimeter. The gate is one of the thickest bars coming to the points at the top to discourage anyone from climbing over. Well, they won't stop me, I say to myself.

The SUV goes around a fountain in the middle of a gorgeous courtyard with a path that goes off to the right into some trees that I think leads into the forest. As the car swings in front of the main stairs leading up with gargoyles guarding either side of the stairs at the bottom on stone pedicles. The stone railing and supports lead up to a beautifully crafted ten-foot-tall wood door with large iron hinges.

Getting out, I am amazed that the gargoyles don't come to life to growl at me that I don't belong here. The driver continues to the other side I assume to some kind of castle garage or stable. Mason calls over his shoulder that he has something to check on before he uses his speed to getaway. The door swings heavily on its hinges, remaining open for Eric and me to come in.

Gulping down the anxiety that is building, I walk up the stone step to the door, that at further assessment carries some scars of its own. The gashes tell of a battle that may have gone bad but I knew not to ask for to pry into the past isn't always good. The mental shiver that goes down my spine, I hope was unseen by those around me.

I place my hands on the strap on my bag that is crossed over my body to keep my hands from wandering. As we enter the castle into a large foyer of luxury, I stop, trying to take in the heavily framed paintings of past kings and queens I assume for they have the look of royalty. The walls are of stone with furniture lining the hall of some benches and tables that have knick-knacks that could pay my rent for years. Why do they have these things just in plain view? My eyes come to a center table in the foyer that has a large clear vase of black roses on a velvet red cloth. Walking to the other side I see that the hallway goes to another set of stairs that lead up to a massive walkway going in either direction and also another ten-foot door with more scars to prove how long it has been there.

I look at Eric for some direction on what we are going to do or even where we are going. He turns to me saying. "We are going to go to the left at the top of the stairs into the future king's wing. I suggest you not wander off while you are here until you have been shown around and the other occupants are aware of you. There is no need for trouble to find you." This did sound fair but I better not make any promises. I am never one to resist the chance to explore even when I know it isn't a good idea. I just can't help myself.

Looking up at the direction he has pointed to, I weigh my options before saying. "I will try not to wander off if that helps?" Smiling up at him I can see he is trying not to smile back at me.

Instead, he starts his way up the stairs not even waiting to see if I would follow. I run after him trying to keep up with his long strides. As he opens the door to the king's wing I am surprised to see all the modern touches.

The floor is a warm deep mahogany wood that softens the stone walls that have beautiful paintings that I am pretty sure are not knock-offs.

Some are Monet, others look to be from Leonardo Da Vinci himself. They look to be behind protective glass frames of black bronze. The rug is in rich colors that vary from deep red to rich blue with all the other colors in between mixed into the intact pattern of inspiration. Going down the hall that opens up to a grand living room with large white couches that one can just sink into with a good book or for a nap. It faces a large fireplace that I could walk right into. The Stone inside has seen many fires over the years.

To sit down there with a fire burning would be pure magic.

We go off to the right to a door that opens to a study or office. The big desk dominates the wall on the far end, as I look at Lucas standing up from behind it.

Seeing him coming around the desk I feel the need to not just run to him but to run from him. I step back but the door I bump into is already shut and I didn't realize that Eric didn't come in with me.

This feels weird.

Why didn't he come in or better yet what am I doing here? Reaching behind myself I tried to open the door but Lucas had other ideas in mind. He places his hand on the door holding it in place all the while he hooks his arm around my waist. Gasping at not the speed at which he got to me but at the closeness of the sexy man that now has me. "Where do you think you>re going my imp? You just got here and I am not ready to let you go as of yet." Lucas purrs into my ear taking a long inhale of my neck before he reaches my ear to purr into.

Closing my eyes and swallowing the lump in my throat I try to keep my breathing at a normal rate. The fact that he is a vampire crosses my mind as he leans in kissing my pulse on my neck. My breath hitches for a second as he releases the kiss from my neck. Looking in those blue steel eyes, I see the smallest bit of red around the Iris.

Lifting my hands onto his chest I applied a bit of pressure to get him to move back. The slow smirk of his lips to the right side of his lips was one of pure devilish intent. I pushed harder at his rock-hard chest, dipping my head to move to the side. His strong arm is unyielding to my move keeping me in place against the door. "Ok, you have proven your point. Now let me go." I say not looking up into his face, as I know now if I do, the pulse I just calmed down would go back up.

After another second he slowly backs away. "So be it but I don't think this is truly what you want judging by that increase of pulse and the dilation in your eyes." Hearing him say this was startling, for he is right.

Shit, I hate it when other people can read me so well. Even if being a vampire gave him an advantage over normal people. It still irked me. Rolling my shoulders to relieve the tension building up, I stepped to the side going over to the sofa to sit before my legs gave out. My body is not used to all this up and down. Ok, to be fair I just wanted to wrap myself up in him.

Crap! Down girl, I say to myself as I sit in the corner of a dark brown leather couch with bronze studs on the front of the chair arms and in the place of buttons for the tufts. Sinking into the soft leather I could feel the cool leather that felt natural against my skin.

It is weirdly comforting.

As I look up I see him studying me almost in fascination, but suddenly his face shuts down behind a frown. He walks over and again sits in front of me on the coffee table. I am happy with the masculine architecture of it. It didn't even groan when his full weight was on it. I start to pull my legs up to hug them but he places his hands on my knees forcing them back down. "There is no need to withdraw from me. I would never hurt my mate," he said this so casually like a breath that goes in and out without the constant need to tell the lungs to draw the next breath or to let it go.

Taking a breath, I say "I am not withdrawing from you. Nor am I afraid of you. I hug things for comfort, like my legs or a blanket on my lap. This seems to calm my mind and body." Wow! I can't believe I told him this.

I keep sharing things that only Tori and Chloe know about me. Why in the world would I share these things with him? Those weird details that a person usually keeps to themselves or if you know someone long enough you just know things by instinct. Like Tori and her morning ritual of diesel coffee or Chloe with her borrowing of clothes, thinking they are hers. Rolling my shoulders back I try to scoot further back into the couch to get some space from him. Yep, that didn't work at all. His long legs cage mine in. Keeping me in place.

Well, I guess I might as well get to it then.

He leans forward onto his knees with his elbows and his arms outstretched with his hands resting on my legs. He slowly moves them up leaning for me. Shit, what the hell is going on with this guy? We just met. Placing my hands on his stopped his progression up my legs. "Ok, you need to give me some space. I have no idea what is going on with us but why do you keep calling me your mate?" I say exasperated. The slow burn in my lower belly was spreading, making my pulse increase from the want of his touch.

His slow grin was mesmerizing. The hint of that bad boy that I think is not just a look comes through as he says. "Haha, you are so cute when you get flustered. Your eyes have a certain shadow that shows up, deepening the color. And that blush just adds to that glow." I reach up to my burning cheeks to discover that this is true but shit, this is not going the way it needs to. "I guess we should start with the fact that you are my mate. The connection that we feel is just the beginning. You have already witnessed that by touching I can help you with your gifts and expand them. I have done some research on the fact that when a vampire finds his mate they not only have to be compatible but very powerful. That way when the mated pair will survive the union. So this goes back to my first question. What are you?" To hear all this and then that godforsaken question is just too much.

I push his hands off. Jumping up I walk around to the other side of the coffee table to start pacing back and forth. Great news! I am turning into Tori! Stomping my foot I turn to Lucas. "I can't tell you what I am. It is not important. Why the fuck do you think I will believe what you are saying? I just met you. So far I have no reason to trust you other than this feeling of a connection." Huffing, I stand there with my arms crossed.

He slowly gets up grabbing me by the arm and drags me to a book that is open on his desk. Pointing at the text of this book I can see that this is not an ordinary book. The Pages are made from old linen paper that is yellowed over time. Some of the writing is faded and the letters are written in old calligraphy. I can't help but read what is in front of me.

The mating bond will be evident in the thread seen linking the two together. To be able to confirm this one must go to an empath. They will be able to read the mated pair to confirm this. Another factor that will help is how the gifts of the two are affected by touching or even eventually being in the vicinity of their mate in the future. When a vampire finds its mate there will never be another being that will come to replace that one. The mate will either be another vampire or a

powerful being made by the Gods themselves. They need to be mated and will become unbearable until the pair succumb to it.

After reading a short part of the book I turn to face Lucas who is standing next to me. I lean back to get a better view of this vampire that is supposedly my mate. My mind goes to an idiotic place of thinking at least he is hot.

Haha yeah, I'm nuts.

Taking a deep breath, I finally can say. "Where is Eric, you said he is an empath? Don't give me that look, I need to hear this from the horse's mouth, so to speak. Get him back here right now," Getting up in his face or as close as I can get to it I let my temper come out. He steps back holding his fingers up to his lips. The whistle was ear-shattering. What the fuck! I duck holding my ears. He just shrugs. "I told my brother to stay close." I can't believe the future king of the vampire's whistles. I know my mouth is hanging open. As he reaches out he grazes my bottom lip with his thumb gripping my chin. I close my mouth sharply then pull back walking around to the front of the desk.

As I lean against the desk the door swings open as Eric comes in. The look on his face as he assesses us is one of a cat that caught the mouse. I'm guessing he must have said something like this was going to happen and Lucas didn't believe him. Yeah, I can relate to that. Before he can cross the room Lucas bellows. "Tell her what you can see. Yes, you were right. Get on with it."

Looking at Eric, I can see the flash of a knowing smile before he walks up to me. I wish I could back up more but to do that would involve me climbing onto the massive desk at my backside. I better just face the music, I guess. "For this to fully work I need you to take some of your shields down so to speak. My gift is very powerful but I think whatever you are is even more so." He said this in a low voice that was so soothing. I felt the need to do so. Shit, this is not good.

Pushing away from the desk, shaking my head trying to clear it was not working. This isn't right. How the fuck, am I to just do this. "How much do I have to let you in?" I know my voice sounds like a whiny child almost but frankly, I don't care. He looks me straight in the face with such compassion. "Just a few, I won't go any deeper than I have to. You have my word." A vampire's word is not something I can easily trust. I have no idea what they are capable of or if they can be trusted.

All right I better just suck it up. "Fine, is there anything else?" I ask. I turned to him for more instructions. Having him look at me was like being under a microscope. "No, that is it. Lucas goes stand next to her," he says to Lucas pointing at the spot next to me. His arm brushes against mine, sending a tingle up. God's above I just wanted him to touch me again. What is wrong with me? How many times am I going to ask this in one day?

Ok, I close my eyes and start to breathe on an even plane. Blocking out everything I concentrate mentally picturing some of my walls to come down. I never thought I would have to take these down. The first one was hard but the next two were not. These have been in place for years. The first one was just a new one I made to hide the wings in my aura. I guess the cat is out of the bag now. Ok, just a little more. I clench my jaw and with the last effort, I can take down those last two. Sweat trickles down my temple. I quickly swipe it away looking off to the side. Looking back to Eric I say. "Ok, I am ready." Lucas slips my small hand into his. Running his thumb up and down my thumb. "Get on with it Eric, we have much to do," he says.

Eric's gaze was penetrating as he turned his gift on us. I could feel small caresses that were so gentle they were like a small breeze ruffling my feathers. It almost felt good until suddenly the caress grew more intense to the point it felt like sandpaper. Shi, that hurts what the hell he is doing.

"Stop!" I am breathing heavily at the abuse from his gift. His gaze locks to mine and I gasp when I see the shock. His mouth moves to say something but nothing comes out. He steps back from us for a moment before spinning back around looking at me again. "You are more than you seem. Brother this woman is your mate. I could see the connection even before she dropped her walls but after I was able to see the full extent. You are already corded together just by being close to each other. There is no one better suited for you Lucas than her. Already her gifts are reaching out to you and yours to her. I think with this happening, both of your gifts will be able to be enhanced by the other, or in your case Alex solidified inside yourself. This will help in coming to full maturity. Yes, I can sense the changes in you and I know what they are."

I am taken aback by this. I try to pull my hand away but Lucas won't let go. I need my space right now but the stubborn man won't let go. Looking up he frowns down at me. "Stop trying to get away from me. You are mine!" The force at which he says this causes me to stop struggling to get my hand back.

He leans down, taking my face into his other hand. I can't help but meet him as our lips crash together. Letting him take the kiss deeper by tilting my head back further. I hear Eric clear his throat. In response, Lucas growls before breaking our kiss. Panting we pull back from each other. What the hell. We let go of each other. "Ok, what the hell are we doing? We barely know each other. You are saying that because of this mate thing we have no choice but to be together?" I say. Lucas suddenly is in front of me again. With his intense stare boring into me I can see that not only has he already accepted this but he was not going to let me go.

Eric puts his hand on his brother's shoulder pulling him back from me. I can see the anger flash across his face before he turns on his brother. "Do not do that again." He growls out at him. Putting his hands up, Eric steps back. "There's more for you to know brother. I have found out why she was not willing to tell us what she is. For her species was thought to be gone. She is not just made by the Gods but made by Odin himself. She is a Valkyrie." he announces this, causing me to gasp. "No, you can not know this! Please stop." I say this last part at a whimper as the feeling of dread pulses through my body. No one is to know this.

I feel the penetrating gazes of the two vampires in front of me. Finally looking up I can see that they are in shock at the discovery of me. "How did you know?" I ask. Eric first looks at Lucas. Lucas nods his head to him, giving him the go-to explanation. "In your aura, wings are protruding from your back, and reading your soul I can feel the Godly presence. Do you have wings?" The wonder in his voice drives me to show them. I reach down pulling my shirt off. "What the hell are you doing? Put that back on!" Lucas lunges to pick up the sweater I have thrown on the ground. I quickly turn, showing them my new tattoos on my back before calling my wings out.

Letting them out felt so good and right. I hate having to put them away. I stood there for a second before turning back around. Meeting their dumbstruck eyes was priceless.

"Guys snap out of it. Yes, I am a Valkyrie and the reason I smell differently from others is that I have part of Odin in me, passed to me by my mother. The other reason is I am in the final stages of my coming of age. This is when my gifts are to be at their full power and abilities." Rushing that out I flex my wings. I continue holding up my hand to make them let me continue. "I am not the only one. My two friends are also Valkyrie's. We are the last of our kind and we have been hiding since the massacre of our people when we were children. You are not to tell anyone about us or I will kill you both." Stepping forward I create an ice blade. Pointing it at them both I get into a fight stance. "Do I make myself clear?" I ask.

Lucas's face turns from a frown to a half-smile for which he uses like the sword in my hand. Seeing his face soften some I lower the sword. "You are truly beautiful and one of a kind. You are mine! The Gods have given me a mate that will be more than one of a kind but one truly destined to be my queen." He says with such pride. This makes me take a step back. "Look I am still figuring this all out. Let's back this up some. I mean we haven't even gone on a date. Not to mention my friends and I are trying to figure out what will happen on my birthday." I hear myself rambling but I have no idea how to stop.

Letting go of the sword I walk away from them. Holding my head, I sit on the couch racking my nails on my scalp. I finally look up and see that Lucas has moved to the coffee table once again boxing me in. Flattening my wings, a bit to lean back. He reaches out to my wings brushing a few into a place that got a little ruffled. His touch is making me crave him to pet me. Literally, pet me. I have no idea but that is what my crazy self is craving.

Lucas leans in more. Caressing a knuckle along my cheek. I grab his hand pulling it away. "Say something." I simply state. I look at him with wide eyes that contain a small plea within. Leaning back, he finally says. "We are meant to be. I can feel this with every fiber of my being. I am to be the next king and you will be my queen. " He holds up his hand to stop me from another protest. "There will be time for you to get used to this but in the meantime, we will get to know each other. No one outside this room will know that you are a valkyrie but I think they will soon know. My kind is very prospective and you are under my protection as my soon-to-be mate. No one will risk my wrath at trying to take you away from me." This arrogant statement was one I just couldn't take to the bank. "You may think this but my kind is dead for a reason. Some powerful people took it upon themselves to do this. We don't even know the reason why." I get this out but I can't help but flashback to that fateful day when I saw my mother for the last time.

I see my mother's face. She was the last we saw of our kind. The beautiful wild raven black hair streaming behind her as she ran to us playing in the backyard. Her face is caked in horror as she runs the rest of the way to us. I run the rest of the way to her as my friends follow behind me. We were always together. She leans down, encircling me in her arms. As my friends catch up they are pulled forward into her arms. "You need to run. Go now. Hide. Do not come back. For one day you will be our salvation." She rushes this out. The push to the back gate is one of desperation but I hesitate to listen to my mother. "But why mother? Where is dad?" My small plea is followed by Tori and Chloe asking about their parents as well. My mother looks over her shoulder as the first of many homes are set aflame. "You three are our last hope. Do not worry about us we will come to find you." She said this while a tear ran down her cheek. She never cries.

Whipping the tear out of the corner of my eye I focus on the present.

I put my wings away and my sweater back on. Sitting there with these two staring at me is somewhat unnerving. "You guys have got to stop staring at me like I am an animal at the zoo," I say. Trying to lighten the mood I give Lucas a small smile. In return, I was gifted with one of his hot sexy bad boy grins. If he keeps doing that I will need a change of panties.

I lay my head back looking up at the stone ceiling with large dark wooden beams. This place is so masculine, so ....him. I bet he doesn't even own a pink shirt. Sighing, I decide to push all of this aside. "Ok now that we know that I am your potential mate." I say holding up my index finger to stop them both from interjecting, "Is this the reason why you brought me here? Or wouldn't let me up to my place? Or here is one to top the list of why I can't call my friends? " Pausing for a second I get no response. "Guys pick one of the questions. Anyone, I don't care about the order you answer them in, as long as all of them get answered." I say testily.

Lucas leans forward again resting his elbows on his knees. He ran his finger up my leg to my knee causing me to shiver. "Are you cold we can get you a blanket?" He asks with a knowing smile. Blushing I say. "I am fine, thanks." This man is going to drive me insane and I just met him. Looking back up I arch my eyebrow indicating for him to continue. So glad he got my hint, for he says. "Ok let's start with don't get upset but when you were at the library your friends had come down to the bar to have coffee but they were ambushed. My guard was not able to hold them off. They were taken and we don't know where. Contacting them would be pointless as their phones were found in ditches on the side of the next block. We will get your friends back. I can't believe someone has taken them but my guard came too recently and said they were upset that they didn't get all three of you at once." As he finished, I couldn't control my anger any longer. I stood up abruptly holding an ice dagger at the base of his neck. I had one knee on top of his left leg and the other one braced to lunge forward to push the blade into his throat. Leaning in close I see the surprise before I am flipped over on the couch with my hands above my head. "Umph," I say as his weight settles on me, pinning me to the couch with no chance of escape.

I need to work on my defense moves because this is embarrassing. I try to squirm out of his hold but this just brings me more under him. "Are you done? I asked you not to get upset. We will help you get them back but this anger is not going to help us. Calm down and I will let you up. Mason is already checking with some of our contacts and Eric will be doing the same. As for us, I thought we could look into anything recently that has happened to you and your friends that would trigger a kidnapping. Is this going to work for you?" That last part was more than a little bit forced down. He is going to lose that temper of his if I am not careful. "Eric go!" He orders not taking his eyes off of me.

I hear the door click behind him and shit we are alone. My breathing is getting more worked up the longer he has me in this hold. I look frantically to the right of me to see if I can try to flip him off but one of his legs is braced on the ground to prevent that. Smart man....."You can get off me now. I won't slice your throat anytime soon I promise." I try to get my upper half up. He adjusts his hold so only one of his hands is holding me and the other takes the dagger away chucking it in the stone wall. It explodes into shards clinking to the stone floor. I jump at the impact of the noise.

His frown line between his eyebrows is back making me want to smooth it out. "Woman, you test me. Why would you want to kill your mate? If you want to fight, then I am all game but let's do that in the training area." God's that smirk as he finishes his smart-ass comment heats the inside me.

I rub my thighs together trying to get some kind of relief. Looking up into his intense face I can see that my movements have not gone unnoticed. "If you continue to squirm like that we are going to get to know each other very quickly. Once I start down that road I have nits intention of holding back my little imp," he says this dipping down nipping at my lower lip and then nuzzling my neck. OMG! That feels so good. My chest rises with every part that he touches. I close my eyes, gulping down the knot in my throat. "Judging by your elevated breathing, I do believe you are getting wet for me, my dear Alex." His smile peels back over his descending fangs by my ear. He then starts to play with my ear. As he bites down a small moan is released from my lips. I feel him reposition himself between my legs holding me down with the weight of him. I can feel his erection through our clothes. Shit the ache in my clit from not getting the release that it craves is unbearable. Moaning again, I finally can open my eyes. Seeing his face above mine with his eyes half-closed over the dark red eyes finally jars me. I push my head back trying to put some distance between us. "We have to stop!" I say but my voice catches, giving away my fear.

I see annoyance in his eyes as he slowly comes back, receding the beast back into himself. "Woman, you will drive me to the brink and back. I will heed this time but next time I don't think the beast will be able to resist you. I have never been this tempted before in my existence." He says, taking one more nip at my bruised lips. For they were thoroughly begging for more of it.

His release of my wrists gave me the ability to prop myself up on my elbows. His movements were stiff and still aggressive as he got off of me. I do believe he has a serious case of blue balls. Smiling to myself I released a small chuckle about his situation. I just can't help it for I have something similar but my ache is not as noticeable as the bulge in his pants is. Haha yeah, that may teach him to not start things that will be interrupted.

The frown over his shoulder at me is a tell of him noticing my chuckle at his expense. I hold up my hands shrugging at him. "You may think this is funny imp, but next time there will be only you begging me to take you." His for sure attitude with the dominance rolling off of him takes me back a step. I surge up off the couch with my temper coming to the surface. "What makes you so sure that you will ever be able to get me to do that? I may feel the pull as much as you but I for one have self-control." Smirking, I hold my ground for one second before going to my phone.

CHAPTER 12

S itting back down I start to scroll through my contacts and jobs that we have done in the past. The only issue is that the one that keeps jumping out at me is Kyro Industries. "I can't seem to get Kyro Industries out of my head. Yes, I know we just had a run-in with them but think about it no other client has been this persistent with its demands or this vague about what and who we are hunting before.

Usually, we have one meeting and then we go about our way of doing things to get the job done. These guys have been very persistent in keeping their company in the dark and on coming along, to get the experiment that was stolen." I say. Getting up from the couch again I go over to the desk where he is working on his computer. He glances up from the laptop but then swings around for me to look at. What the?..... I know this file. Looking up at Lucas I say. "How did you get these files? We had to hack into their database to get these files on them." Leaning over to examine more of the files that he has, he says. "We were able to clone your feed and look at whatever you were looking at. I also was able to get deeper into their bank accounts. They have a lot of money that they are trying to hide." Scanning over this I can see a pattern in when the withdrawals are happening. "If you look at the amount it is always under $10,000. This way they are not flagged by the government. But if they can make these kinds of withdrawals then why are they operating in the red?" I pointed this out to him on the laptop. Turning it to face him I see a light go off in his head. "The bank that they are using is one of the banks out of Seattle but I can get us access to the accounts. The owner is a good friend." The sheen in his eyes and the way his voice deeps at the word friend is not comforting.

Straightening up I walk away from him to get my thoughts in order. I can't stop thinking about what we almost did and I still want to do. I try to mentally shake myself out of it. My friends are in trouble. I can feel them deep down, for that connection is only severed when one of us dies. Rubbing that spot on my chest where the sorceress performed this connection to them I got an idea. I think I can use this spot on my chest to fuel my gift into taking me to either the past or future of them. I just wish I knew which one would take me too. Gods above this if so frustrating.

Racking my hands through my hair I feel an arm come around me pulling me in to face him. "I see the wheels turning in that brain of yours. What have you come up with?" Lucas asks. Shifting to break free of his hold once again, I then say. "We had a sorceress forge a connection to each other a few years ago when one of us went out on a job but didn't come back when we were supposed to." Looking down, I think he can guess who that was. "When this happened the other two went a little crazy because they didn't know if the other was dead or not. The thing is, I received a part of them myself and they did this vice-versa. If I can latch on to this, I may be able to go to the future or the past to see where or what is happening."

Now beaming at the idea, that I said out loud solidified that I needed to try this.

Ok, I start to center myself inward. Reaching for that space that my friends occupy within me. I see the light of their auras shining out at me. One greenish-blue for Chloe and Tori was of white light with swirls of the storming greyish blue going through the white. Letting them shine even brighter, I grasp onto them letting my aura mingle with theirs. I feel Lucas feeding some of himself into me like he did before and I was again able to concentrate more freely on bringing forth the past or future. Feeling the tug forward, I leap through time to the future or present.

I look around myself seeing that I am in an old space that has been abandoned for years. The windows are cracked or boarded up because they have been broken years ago. The walls were dirty and covered in years of dirt. But in this small room on the scarred wooden floor, I see that my friends are tied to some chairs. I rush over to them realizing we must be in some kind of office area with storage. There are a lot of crates, boxes, and shelves in the small space. The years of dirt, dust, and decay are very prominent. On the surfaces that surround us. As I get closer, I start to take in that they were unconscious.

Shit, I hope that they can see me like the last time I went into a vision. I reach out to Chloe to touch her shoulder but my hand passes through her. Crap this is just like old-time visions I guess. "Chloe, can you hear me? I need you to wake up." I say in a whisper by her ear. I don't want to draw anyone in here even if they couldn't see me they may be able to hear me.

After a second or two, I leaned back from her. Studding the area again I walk over to the windows. I try to see through the grime on them but it is too thick. I continue along with the windows until I get to an actual hole in the plywood from one of the windows being broken.

I look out to find that the building is not an office building but an old abandoned school. I see broken play equipment below. The rungs of the ladder for the slide rusted out in some areas causing them to fall off or simply hang there. The slide itself had a hole at the bottom from years of collecting water with the rust eating away at it. The weeds and trees trying to take over the climbing gym were ones of beauty and horror. The swings only had chains hanging down, with vines growing up the poles. Wow looking at the rest of nature taking back what is it's own was startling.

Shuttering one last time at seeing the seesaws broken or completely gone from decay I turned back from the scene to find that I needed to leave them to find them. Taking that deep breath, I go back into myself willing to go back to the present.

Blinking the fog away from the outer ring of my vision, I came fully back into myself. Looking into Lucas's face I can see the crease in between his brows so I reach up without thinking to smooth it out. Just as I am about to touch it I suddenly come to my senses freezing just before. I pull it back down looking away quickly. Breathing out, I step back but his hold remains in place. "Let go of me," I say, shrugging in his grasp, trying to shake off his hands. He just grips me tighter, pulling me up to him to look into my eyes. "No. I like the way you feel and I didn't know if you were going to stay upright this time. What did you see in your vision? Did you go to the past or the future?" His demeanor of authority didn't change through this but his grasp did lighten to something not as aggressive as he got this out.

I recall him trying to get this out of me during the vision but I was too busy in the vision to pay attention to him. I knew I was present so there was no need to worry. So, I tried to relax in his grip as much as possible. "I went to either the future or a side step to where they are. I could feel you the whole time it was a strange sensation. If you are up for it can you feed me some of your magic? I want to see what happens." I know asking this is a big thing. Doing this would prove the connection even more but at this point, I didn't care.

Seeing the surprise in his eyes at my request was like a person getting a present. The joy behind it is one that a person gets after opening up a present. I will give this connection a chance for my friends. If it helps them then so be it.

I lean forward to him saying. "Can you lean down? It might help if our foreheads touch. I also want to see if you can see what I am seeing this time. I ask that you try harder this time to not go any deeper." Lifting my right eyebrow, I look up at the shock on his face. I know he will try something again if given the chance so maybe a pre-warning will help discourage this. "I will try to resist the temptation of your beautiful mind. I just want to get to know my mate," he says. Sighing, I shrug. "This may be true but let's try the old-fashioned way of asking questions and letting the whole natural thing of getting to know each other go first," I said, giving him a half-smile and crossing my arms over my chest waiting for him.

Looking into his eyes, I start to feel the slight pressure on my mind as he starts to probe for an opening. I slowly take a deep breath and slowly let it out. As I let out my breath, I push my walls down letting him in just under the surface. I moan at the caress I feel as he enters into the outer reaches of my mind. "Ok, here goes nothing," I say. Pulling at the spot in my chest I let their aura, shine bright. My gift pulls me into the vision.

Standing in the room again, I slowly turn to take in my surroundings. The shelves are in place with all the dirt and moldy boxes. I walk around one of the shelves to look at the corner of the room where I had seen my friends earlier. Sure, enough there they are still tied up and unconscious.

I mentally reach back into myself, finding Lucas on the outer reaches. "I think we are in the same spot of time I was earlier. Can you see what I am seeing?" Asking this was weird. I walk over to them once again looking for any change to see if I am for sure at the right time. I hear Lucas speaking but it is too faint so I suck it up and let down another wall of my mental barriers. Hearing him finally was a relief but weird. I am willing to let this vampire in. Something that I thought I would never do, with anyone, let alone my mate. Shit, why am I thinking about this right now? This is really bad timing. Ok, concentrate Alex!

After my mental slip and pep talk, I focus on what he is saying. "Alex, I can see what you are but can you get to the windows to see outside?" He asks. I quickly move to the spot in the broken plywood that I found earlier. "This is where I looked out earlier, but I don't recognize this school or day-care facility. Do you know where this place is? It looks pretty run down." Talking to him in my head is weird. I physically try to keep the shutter down my spine in check. "I think I have an idea of where this is. I think that is all we need to do here." He says this receding back from my mind I also slowly step back from the vision. Taking one last look at my friend's.

We come too, still grasping each other and foreheads still touching. Inhaling some of his scent, I pull back taking some time to get my bearings. He finally let's go of me. I quickly walk away putting some distance between us as I try to build back up my walls. I can't go walking around here with my mind open. I have learned that you cannot trust everyone you meet. Mentally shaking myself once again, for I am not going back to that day ever again.

I walk back over to his desk. Looking over his shoulder, I can see that he has some maps of the city pulled up. "Judging by the growth of the trees and that amount of growth on the playground equipment, I believe that it is in this area here East of town. If you go out of town about 20 or 30 miles you will run into this old abandoned town. No one, to my knowledge, lives there but I do believe it is haunted." As he explained this I think to myself that it is weird to see a town with no name on a map. "What was the name of this town? Why is it empty? I get that it is a secluded place but there are plenty of those here in town." Saying this I start to think of all the places that we stayed in when we were homeless trying to hide and get by. Taking a breath, I look at the screen again, as he starts clicking some of the areas that have been documented by google earth.

As he gets closer to the edge I see what could pass for a football field or an area for soccer. Pointing at the screen I say. "I think I found the school. Over there by the woods, there looks to be a football field and that could be the playground. Is there a picture of the front of this building?" I need to calm down but I just know this is the place. I just can't believe that they are there. He touches the screen pulling up an old photo of the school when it was just beginning to be taken back by nature.

Reading the sign out loud. "Gifted Academy" I stand back trying to think if I have ever heard of this school but alas nothing comes to mind. Just like the town. "I have never heard of this school before and it doesn't give us what the town is called either." Stepping back, I lean my head against the bookcase muttering. "This fucking sucks." I feel that his eyes are on me and sure enough when I tip my head forward, I see those intense steel blue eyes on me. "There may not be the name of the town in that school but I do believe I have heard of that school before. Some of our kind helped to build it. It was only open for a few short years before it suddenly closed and then people started to die.

No one knows what happened in that town but I can tell you that if the few who moved away can be found then we will be able to get that information. For now, let›s go get your friends." He holds out his hand to me after getting up from his desk chair.

Looking at the outstretched hand, I can't but help feel the pull to take it. I place my hand in his, as he walks us back to the couch. Sitting on the lush fabric again I can't help but blush a little over what we almost did. "We need to get there as soon as possible but I think we will take a few of my men with us. I would like it if you stayed here but I have the feeling that you won't do that." I want to roll my eyes and say *duh* to him. Instead, I look him dead in the eye and say. "You are right, I am not going to leave my friends and besides I think you can use my help." He clears his throat ever so slightly moving back in his seat. "I was more worried about your safety and I don't think you will like how we take care of some of these men." His statement is said through clenched teeth barely holding back the growl that can be heard through his words. "I have seen and heard a lot in my short life, so don't worry about me." I may be cocky but I am right. Leaning back, crossing my arms over my chest. I hope this looks more intimidating than I think it does. He does make everyone else in the room look small with his big muscles and strong features. I bet many men just curl up and cry when he unleashes his temper.

After a few more seconds of us just staring each other down, he picks up his phone. I can only hear his side of the conversation but it sounds like we will be moving out soon and we will have some backup coming with us. This is good because I didn't want to have to get my other friends involved in this. They already think our business is dangerous and sometimes sketchy. Some days we almost have them back down to a normal concerned level but with everything happening lately, they are getting back up to that. I will intervene or tie you to a chair if you do any more dangerous jobs attitude. It gets old real fast. Thankfully I love them so I can't get too mad at them.

After he hangs up I see some of the strain in his eyes and I reach for him instinctively. Holding his hand, I tried to fuel some of my *we got this* to him. "How long till we leave? I think it might be a good idea to have some kind of plan." I say getting up to go to the door. In a second, he is standing in front of the door. "You need to stay in this room right now. The other vampires need to be instructed on who and what you are. Your species is not just rare but powerful. I know some about your kind but just knowing that you are my mate will adhere to you. You are not just a rare beauty but one that will be hunted once it gets out." Says Lucas. How can he know this? I barely have been able to find information on why we were slaughtered and we have no idea who did it. "Do you know why my people were slaughtered?" My temper was up and I am ready to fight for answers. "I know that twenty years ago there were more of you and before that there were even more spread out over the continents. Suddenly for 100 years or so your people were being hunted and taken. I don't know who was doing this but I can help you find out." His declaration cooled my temper a few notches.

"We were a part of a small group of people that were hiding. One day we were playing in my yard when my mother came to us yelling for us to run. Run and don't look back. One of us will meet you at the stream but if we are there for more than a day then we are to continue without them. We waited for two days but we could not listen to our families to keep going. We needed to see what happened to them. Why didn't anyone show up?" A tear ran down my face.

Lucas was instantly there catching the tear as it rolled down my cheek. He brought the tear up to his lips tasting it. "Your tears taste like the sun and the sky." Lucas closes his eyes like he is savoring the taste before he says something further. "You should have listened to your mother because those people could have still been there." I stepped back from him pushing on his chest. Which of course did nothing, as he has muscle on top of the muscle. "We were kids! We all wanted to see our families again. When we got there, our homes were ash and all the animals were dead. Not a soul was found until we came to the center of our little town.

They had set the bodies on fire to erase what they had done. Judging by the amount of ash and that of the flames that were still burning not all were there. We think some had been taken. I was able to have a vision but the only thing it showed me was the flames and people screaming." Shutting my eyes, I try to push the images and the sounds back into the corner of my mind where I keep those I wish to forget. I still have nightmares with flames that are never-ending and of my people burning. "We were able to get to the next town claiming asylum." Flinching at this, I then said, "I can't get into this right now."

Taking a shuddering breath, I look into the eyes of Lucas, seeing not pity but pure anger. I can see the red coming through and his fangs descending as he growls out his anger. "I will protect you. No one will ever get that close to you ever again." His declaration was made out of possession and anger. I felt the heat of his anger towards those who wish me harm as a caress of comfort. The only other people to have that kind of effect on me were my friends but they have lived through the same horror that I have.

His phone goes off causing us both to take a step back. I can see him fighting for control over his anger. Reeling it back in he grabs his phone from his pocket. "Yes! Is everything ready? ...No I want this done quickly. Do not argue with me. I know this will be dangerous. We will be down momentarily." Lucas says all this then angrily hangs up still trying to get his temper in check. I tentatively walked over to him. Reaching up I put my hand on his cheek. "I thank you for your anger and not your pity. For pity is not something I welcome. We are stronger than most and will one day find out what happened to my people. Until then please try to remember that I am right here and am strong. I can take care of myself and what is mine." My face is set in a stern but a soft voice to back it up to get that I cared for the anger he has towards those who have caused me pain.

He pulls my hand down. "It is time for us to go but this conversation is not over imp." His playful name didn't discourage the heat of anger that is still there in his eyes. Shuttering, I turn in his arms to go. He lightly pulls me back. "You are mine and as you say, I protect what is mine," he whispers this in my ear before letting me go. I am pulled along, behind him, through to the living room. I try to pull my hand free when I see Mason and Eric standing there waiting.

Mason looks not too pleased that I am in his brother's grasp and not his. It is weird how much the thought of being in his arms instead, scares the living shit out of me. I hear Lucas growl at his brother causing him to step back and to look down. When he looks back up I see that he is more reserved. "I was able to prove that the land is owned by a shell company but we are still trying to figure out who owns it," Mason said, looking his brother in the eyes before looking to Eric to continue. Taking that as his cue Eric says. "I was able to round up 30 of the guards on this short notice and we can leave 20 here. I believe there is no need to call any of our other men and women in. I also think it is wise to introduce the members of the guard that we have presented to your mate right away so there is no confusion." Eric says, bowing his head and taking a step back.

This can't be happening this fast. I barely have time to process this myself and now they want to just tell everyone. I can't believe this. Looking at Lucas, I not only see that he is about to agree with his brother but the small smile tells me he is happy about it. I start to walk forward but Lucas speaks before I can. "I would say yes to that but I first need to present her to the court before she can be presented to the rest of our people. We need to do this the right way. Her species alone will be a great additive to us but we need to make sure that she can survive it." Hearing him say this I step back. I open my mouth and no words come out. What does he mean to survive it? I am only maturing into my full self-right now. Did he go deeper into my mind? I have to stop letting him in. Ok focus Alex, let's save your friends first then we can get to the surviving it thing.

Stepping back up to the side of Lucas. I tug on his arm to get his attention. "We need to talk about this and you need to stop taking charge of my life. You may be my mate but no one is in charge of me." I said angrily. "Can we go? I do believe that we need to move on this soon. There is no telling what they will do with Tori and Chloe." I start to walk to the door to go but am quickly grabbed by my arm. He swings me around facing him. His intense gaze causes me to pull back into myself. I also try to pull away from his grasp. "You are my mate and I will do whatever it takes to keep your ass safe." The aggression that came out with the last word, drove the statement home. He was going to try to control me but he would fail. I am one stubborn valkyrie! "Good to know. Now can we go save my friends?" I cock my eyebrow up tilting my head to the side waiting. He releases me running his hand through his hair. I guess in frustration for let's face it, he is dealing with me.

I turn to go out the door as Mason and Eric are already at it waiting for us. Going back through onto the balcony I get a pull to the other side but squash it down for it is not the time to explore. We load up into several SUVs. This time I am between Eric and Lucas. They don't leave a girl a lot of room. I tried wiggling my hips to get some more room but this just caused Lucas to snake his arm around me and pull me to him. I didn't even bother with trying to get out of his hold. There is nowhere for me to go and I am pretty sure the guys in the back are getting suspicious of their future king's behavior.

CHAPTER 13

Walking through the dense woods proved to be easier with vampires. One swipe from their clawed hands cleared a pretty good path. One of the guards froze shouting "stop". Mason came over to him at a silent speed that was like a wind going through the branches. He motioned for us to stay put and get down.

Crouching down, behind Lucas was like being behind a wall. A gorgeous wall of muscle. Not bad to look at but still, I wish I could see around him.

Inspecting the woods around me I started to get a sense that it is way too quiet here and the ground looks undisturbed. There should be some disturbance from wildlife. Mason comes back just as quickly but it is too late.

The ground erupts, sending dirt and rock in all directions. What comes out is something from a nightmare. *Decompositions Corpus* are creatures that used to be human but now they are corpses taken over.

A corpse can be turned into this with the right spell or if you have the gift of necromancy. This is a rare gift and one that many people fear. The power of the spell determines how long the corpse is under the master's command but if a necromancer does it then it will last as long as the necromancer is alive.

The decayed flesh on some are to the point of just bones and others were dripping rotten flesh, as they walked for us. I knew from experience that these things are hard to get rid of. Even more so, if it is someone you know that is under this spell.

I think it would be hard to cut and burn your mom or neighbor. Sighing, I try to get my shit together. Looking at Lucas and the others I see that they are not going to wait for those things to get to us.

Without hesitation I see the vampires change into their true selves. Their fangs descend to sharp points that can tear your throat out. The eyes turned blood red giving them that haunted look. Then their faces seem to pale even more with a hardness to them to match their stone muscles.

I shiver at this before calling forth the cold. Drawing it to the surface is becoming easier with each time I use it. Forming a sword made of ice, I step forth around Lucas but he suddenly puts his hand out. "I know that you wish to fight but I can't risk you getting hurt. It is bad enough having you here where there are so many risks." He says this with such concern and heat behind it I take a step back and start to lower my sword.

Looking up at him I finally come to my senses. "I am going to fight! So get used to seeing me beating the crap out of those that get in my way.

Like I said before, I protect what is mine." I sprint forward before he can stop me. Reaching my first walking corpse I go for the head first. It ducks out of the way of my sword bringing his own up, slicing at the air as I dodge him. Out of the corner of my eye, I see Lucas take his arm off. Jumping forward I cut his head off. Lucas's glare is with red eyes, they should make me wet my pants but instead, I just tilt my head to the side and nod my head in thanks before I dismember the rest of his limbs.

Lucas steps away to take out another. It is weird when you cut into them there is no blood for, they are so far into the decomposition that there is nothing left but the smell these guys give off makes you want to puke. Forcing the bile back down before I move on to my next corpse.

After I get to a second one, I start to see that a few of the guards are setting them on fire, destroying them permanently. I like to think that we are doing them a favor, for who wants their former body walking around in a gross army of death. *Ewe*! It didn't take long for us to get through them all but I think our element of surprise is gone for sure.

We leave the scene of horror behind us. Lucas comes to me, yanking me to him crushing his lips down on mine. I can't help but give it right back before we pull away panting. "I was wrong to try to hold you back. But by all the God's women, you had better not die!" Lucas says this with some force behind it that matches his crown prince title but the heat in those blood-red eyes tells a different story.

Nodding my head, I look then at the guards around us. "Umm, Lucas," I say softly, shifting my eyes to the right to get him to look at his men. He quickly turns to his men. "You are to protect her with everything you have. I will explain later but for now, know this. If any harm is to come to her today there will be hell to pay for those involved." His booming voice was truly scary but I can't help but blush at this declaration. "Ok, now that that is out of the way, can we go save my friends," I say, stepping up to Lucas squeezing his arm. His growl tells me I hit a spot with my brazen comment.

I didn't care because I am not a girl to just cower on the sidelines. I suddenly feel my wings tingling at my back. Looking over my shoulder I feel them coming to the surface so I push the ice in my veins to that part of my back. I hold on to Lucas for support because they are fighting me to get out. "Are you ok? What is going on?" Lucas ducks down to my level shifting back to his regular self, of steel blue eyes and no fangs. "I don't know what is happening. Leave me here, go get my friends. I will come to the fight soon."

Pushing him away I go to the ground to keep pushing the ice. He picked up my ice sword and placed it by my hand. As he turns to go, I see a figure up ahead. "Wait! Who is that up ahead?" Asking this brings everyone to attention, to the figure up ahead that has his hand raised. I feel another pull on my back as his hand goes further up. Shit, this guy is trying to get me to transform. Reaching up I grab Lucas. "The bastard is trying to get me to show who I am. I can't let that happen." Whispering this to Lucas, I see him signal for the attack on the figure up ahead. Arching my back, I feel another person take me from Lucas. Eric speaks to Lucas while taking me from him. "I will take her. Go! Go get the bastards!"

As he continues to pull me back from everyone, I see Mason kill the guy who was trying to pull my wings out. Collapsing into Eric I am out of breath. Eric switched his arm to support me and this is when I see the ice encasing his arm that was touching my back. I gasp trying to pull away not wanting to hurt him. "Don't worry the cold doesn't affect me as much. Haha yes, I do feel it but I am naturally cold as well. Though you may be the coldest creature I have ever touched."

I know he is trying to lighten the mood and get my attention off of what is happening around me. Looking him in the face I say "Thanks, I think they will stay put now." Shifting out of his grasp, I turn to run for the others that have come into the woods. "Go ahead of me. I can take care of myself." Eric glares at me before responding. "I don't wish to have my brother's temper directed at me. Stay by my side till this is over or until Lucas can look after you." Really? This guy too. "I am not some puny human now, get your vampire ass into the fight and stop worrying about me or your brother's temper. If anything, his temper will be directed at me once this is over, for he will know just how I feel about being kept out of a fight." I angrily got this all out before continuing on my run.

As I get to the figure that was trying to get my wings to come out, I notice his outstretched hand. I have to do a double-take. I squat down picking up his hand. I push his sleeve up more so I can see the tattoo on his hand and arm. It is a skeleton hand with roses at the wrist going up his arm. This can't be.

My vision! How is this tattoo on this guy the same as my vision from the past? Shaking my head, I get back up noticing Eric is still there. "This is the same tattoo as my vision. This guy is not the guy from my vision though. He feels different from that guy, but how is this possible?" My shock is not helping my brain to process all this. I take out my phone, snapping a picture of it and him before Eric pulls me along.

I can hear them fighting. It is weird being on the back end of the fight where you can hear all the sounds of a battle. "Eric, I have an idea. They are all busy fighting each other. We can sneak around to get to my friends. There are a few guards at the outskirts that we can grab to come with us." I say this pulling him to the right. "Ok, but you are not to leave my side. I have a feeling this was meant as a trap. They are too well organized for this all to be a simple kidnapping," Eric steps around in front of me calling four of the guards to come with us. Lucas is in the middle of all this but I don't want him to get distracted by us. "Eric, pick me up! We need to move faster!"

I jump into his arms which he then starts to run at a speed I can only dream of. We get around the fight. I look back at it thinking it looks like we are winning. It won't take them much longer to get through to join us.

Looking ahead I see the playground from my vision. But as I scan the playground, I see that there are two figures tied to the merry-go-round. "It is them; they are tied to the merry-go-round!" I shout this getting down from Eric. Just as Lucas comes up to my side placing a protective hand on my shoulder. He nodded at his brother to continue.

I try to shrug his hand off but let's face it he won.

As we get closer a man comes out in a hooded long coat. He raises his hand just like in my vision. "Get her! She is the one I need!" His hand and the skeleton tattoo going up into his sleeve just like the guy back there, but this guy seemed familiar. I am pretty sure he is the one from my vision. Looking at Lucas I can see he thinks the same.

Lucas pushes me behind him. "Stay with me or run!" He looks over his shoulder at me with remorse and anger. As he steps forward, he slices through the neck of one. "Please run!" His plea was one that I wish I could say yes to but I am a Valkyrie and we do not run. "You know I can't!" I simply say coming out from behind him. I can see the respect in his eyes but I also see fear. I think this is a new emotion for this soon-to-be king.

We all start running to meet those that are now pouring out of the school building. I dodge a spray of water before firing one of my little ice spears at her. I catch her in the shoulder but this doesn't deter her for long.

I raise my sword running at her. She in turn gets hers from the sheath at her side. I see that her hand has the skeleton tattoo also before I swing catching her across the neck. I dive to the right to avoid the spray of blood but it caught me a little on the left side.

As I come back up, an arm snakes around my neck, and I feel a dagger pressing into my side. "Don't fight me. I will hurt you." He says in my ear. I try to look for Lucas but he is busy with the three of them. If I call out for help, he might get hurt.

Ok, I need another plan. "Why do you want me? Why take my friends?" I ask these while he slowly walks back to the door that they had come pouring out of. As we get closer, I see the exact moment when Lucas spots that I have been taken. The anger that ripples off of him is potent in the air.

The pure rage has his eyes flashing to reddish-black. He motions his hand to the side causing the door to come off its hinges and hit the man in the back who is holding me. I stumble forward at the impact. The dagger creates a shallow cut, as the man tries to keep his hold on me. The door takes him to the ground.

Righting myself I turn, shooting an ice spear through the man's back as he tries to get up. I turn to my friends but am stopped by the hooded man. He shoots a sound wave at me causing me to be thrown back into the ground.

Ahhh, that fucking hurt! I punch the ground, getting my anger out.

I roll over and try to get up from the ground but feel a foot pressing into my chest. Looking up into him all I can see is a black void inside the hood. I try to push his foot off but he leans forward sniffing the air. "You are the one. Come with me peacefully or I will hurt your friends." His voice sounded like gravel or of someone that smoked all his life.

Pulling my head up I say. "Fuck you! Touch them again and I will kill you!" I take the heel and the toe of his foot, twisting it. This causes him to stumble back trying to avoid the breaking of his ankle. I kick upbringing myself up to his level. His hood comes slightly back revealing his face as he is pushed back from me. It is heavily mutilated on one side with scars from burns. They have long since healed but the skin is no longer white but married with angry red scars. His eyes are black pits that speak of the horrors he will cause me. His hair is long brown that waves in the wind giving him a crazed look. I can see that the tattoo goes partway up to his neck.

He lunges forward trying to get to me but I sidestep him, bringing my elbow to the back of his head as he passes me. He stumbles before righting himself. I look around at his men that are left standing. "What the hell do you want with me?" He takes a step forward, not taking his eyes from me. I raise my sword tilting my head to the side daring him to come closer. He stops but gives me a mutilated smirk that makes me want to puke. His laugh is one that can make even a mother back away. "You are coming with me, that is all you need to know." He says this and then whistles by placing his thumb and pointer in his mouth. I don't know who he just called or signaled to but I am not going with him.

Suddenly the glass from the windows behind me exploded outward letting forth a horde of demons. Not just any but the ones from my vision and the trail at Carson Park.

What the fuck! How the hell do these guys keep getting all of these demons out of hell.

I turn back to Scarface who hits my sword aside, as my shock wears off. He wraps his arm around my waist bringing a knife to my neck, holding me in place. Shit, this was not good. I hear Lucas yell out. "Let her go! I will kill you if you harm her." His roar after this shook the ground and playground equipment. His wings came out pushing him forward. The anger rolling off of him does not deter the man holding me. I feel him chuckle under his breath at seeing the crown prince coming to my aid.

"It is time to leave my pet. "He says under his breath as he backs away. I try to deter him from doing this but the knife digs in and I can feel a trickle of my blood run down my neck. I inhale sharply at the pain. "Don't fight me." His stern voice in my ear was eerie.

I push the cold forth into his arm at my neck. I feel the knife come away slightly. His grip on my waist tightens. I take this advantage in my hands and shoot a small spear of ice into his arm at my waist. He yells out in pain. "Aaahh! You little bitch!" Twisting around to face him I create an ice sword and pull my dagger from the sheath on my thigh. Crouching down I get ready to fight.

He looks down at his arm and pulls the ice spear out with a grunt. The spear is thrown to the side and breaks into a hundred pieces when it hits the floor. "I am not going with you. What do you want with me?" I say blocking the first swing of his sword. Pushing back against him to get a few steps away from him. "My master wants you. He will get you eventually. Just come now and I will spare your friends this time. For next time I will kill them all." He said this with such malice and joy at the word kill, I just wanted to spit in his face.

I look at the fight around me knowing that we were not winning but we were at least not dead. "You may have the upper hand but I think it is time for us to go. Lucas! We need to leave!" Yelling this last part out, I turn to run. I feel a hand try to grab me but he fails. I reach Lucas just as he takes the head off of another demon. He opens his arms, bending down and launching himself into the air. Taking us up away from the fight. I see Mason and Eric each grab one of my friends doing the same. The rest of the guards finish off their opponent before running away in a blur.

I look back over his shoulder at his massive wings. They are beautiful! I settle in his arms absorbing some of his scents. Closing my eyes, I take it in and enjoy the rest of the ride, so to speak.

CHAPTER 14

Being back at his estate feels safe for the moment but my friends were still asleep. Looking down at them on the couches I can't help but focus on the rise and fall of their chests. Seeing the movement of the breathing was helping to settle my Valkyrie side but my wings were again pushing to get out. The tingling at my back was intense but I didn't want to give in. Even though Lucas knew what I was. I still can't let that side of me show. The warning from my mother so long ago was so ingrained in me. *Never show what I am.* I repeat this to myself a few times in my head before walking over to the office door.

I hesitate before I place my hand on the handle of the door. Should I be going in there? Should I take my friends and go? These questions keep rotating in my head. I step back again, taking a few breaths. "There is no need for you to be afraid. Come in." I hear from the other side of the still shut door from Lucas. "Damn those vampire senses."

Going into this room, I try not to look at the couch that we were on last time. Just thinking about what had nearly happened made me blush and shiver at the same time.

Lucas comes around his desk. He leans against it with his legs crossed and his hand resting on the desk behind him. He is not good at playing cool. His intense eyes were following me as I crossed the room. I stop a few feet from him trying to keep some distance between us. I can't keep looking into those eyes. Something about them draws me in and makes me want to get closer to him.

"You are still not going to trust me? It has been proven that you are my mate and your friends are now safe." He shoves off the desk. He is so fast. He grabs me, pulling me forward, spinning me so I am now the one leaning against his desk. I can't help but "gasp". I brace myself on the desk. Looking up slightly I can see the triumph in his eyes. His hand at my back feels like it is trying to imprint itself and my wings push even harder to get free as his hand goes up and down. I try pushing more ice to my back but I feel them surge out behind me. Pushing items off his desk to the floor. I wince at every item that hits the floor before all is quiet once again. The only sound is our breathing and that is slowly building from the intensity between us.

He doesn't even flinch as my wings do damage to his desk. He looks over my shoulder at my wings before crushing his lips to mine. He bends me the rest of the way back to the desk. Swiping the rest of the things from his desk to the floor before shifting his leg between mine. I jump slightly hearing everything hit the floor. Trying to push back but his leg anchors me in place and his lips are doing the best thing to mine.

They are probably the only soft thing about him and the skill at which they move over mine I just can't help but take it in. I grasp some of his shirt in my hands pulling him closer. His hand moves up my neck to the back of my head. I feel him grasp my hair pulling my head back slowly. His lips move from my lips making a trail down to my neck. He sucks slightly before taking a small lick.

I moan out my pleasure.

Wrapping my arms around him, pulling him back up to my lips. He chuckles at me before crashing back down to my lips. His leg moves a little over my core. I gasp at the way my body responds to him. I moan under the onslaught from his lips. Trying to get closer to him.

His hand is under my shirt, working its way up till I finally feel him grasp my breast in his hand. He squeezes it and in return, I arch into his hand for more. He nibbles on my ear as I wither beneath him. "Your response to me is hard to resist my valkyrie but your friends are starting to stir. I think we will be discovered shortly." He chuckles low in the back of his throat as he nips at my throat once again.

Two can play at this game. I nibble his ear lobe, sucking it in before leaning back. I smirk up at him as I see him fighting for control. "Damn it imp!" He says bringing his hand out of my shirt he holds me in place with my hands held above me.

We are both breathing heavily. My core is throbbing for him to continue and looking down at him I can see that he feels the same way. He shoves himself off of me, stalking me with a 'groan'.

I take a moment to get my breathing under control. I slowly pull myself up, first to my elbows, then to a standing position. The whole time I can't help but keep my eyes on him and count the minutes till he touches me again. Looking at my wings, I can see a few of the feathers out of place so I bring them in, smoothing them out. I look at my jacket that is in tatters. I need to get a jacket that can allow my wings to come out without destroying my clothes. Or get strong enough to push through the fibers of the cloth. The strongest supernaturals can do this. It would save a lot on clothes. I shrug my wings back into myself, much to their regret. At the same time, I take off the jacket and toss it aside. Luckily my shirt is mostly ok but still, it will need replacing.

I look to the door, wondering if they were awake. Just thinking about them has me rushing to the door, ignoring Lucas who is growling at my opening the door. 'Tough luck' I think to myself.

I am getting the feeling that he doesn't want me to leave the room or maybe his sight.

Either way, my friends needed me.

They were both sitting up looking pretty good but confused. "Tori! Chloe! You're awake!" I shout. I run the rest of the way to them. We embrace in a three-way hug. "Are you guys ok? What happened? How did you guys get taken?" I rush these questions out looking from Tori to Chloe for answers. They lean back looking at each other. Then Chloe says. "Yes, we are fine. They got the jump on us at the bar and they only tied us up and knocked us out with this sleeping potion." Tori joined in, reassuring me. "We are ok, but how did you find us? And how did we end up in this place?" She sounded more curious than scared of course. She always did like old places....especially ones that even from inside looks like it is a castle.

She will be excited when she finds out that Lucas's estate is a castle. Tori will be impossible to resist the lure to explore.

I hear Lucas clear his throat behind me. "Ummm" Looking over my shoulder he motions with his hand for us to sit down. I try to go sit by my friends but he pulls me down on the opposite couch away from them. The look between them is so weird. I glare up at him as he places an arm around me. "Don't," he simply says out of the corner of his mouth when I try to get back up. This one word from him makes me pause.

It isn't worth the struggle to disobey him on this.

Sighing, I decide to stay where I am. Why make a scene. I leaned back into his arm with his hand gripping my hip. He squeezes it before turning back to my friends. "You were taken because Alex was not there. They were after her, not you. After they had you they simply used you as bait. Alex found you by using her vision power." I take his pause in that he was done.

"My vision power has grown. I can go to the past, present, or future and interact with it. The amount that I am there I cannot control. I need more practice for sure if this happens again and that guy shows up I don't know what to do. I have no idea if he can get to me that way or not." I sigh, throwing my hands up.

Tori leans forward saying. "Why do you think he is after you?" She looks between us before she lights up. "Do you think it has to do with what you are and who you are?" Haha got to hand it to her, for trying to be cryptic but she sucked at this. Her intense stare was shadowed by fear. Chloe put her arm around her, giving her a small hug.

I guess this is as good a time as any. "I think it does, but I also think that we need to keep a low profile for you guys could be in trouble, if they figure you guys out too." I look at them and then back at Lucas. Chloe and Tori look at me and just nod their heads. I turn to Lucas. "I am not the only Valkyrie left. Tori and Chloe are also Valkyrie. We are from a village that was destroyed but we think some of our kind were taken also... but most were killed." I say all this calmly as I can but, on the inside, I am freaking out.

When I finish this, I hear a gasp and something being knocked over. Looking over I see Eric and Mason standing there. They both look shocked but Mason's face changes to one of deep thought, that I don't like. I sink into Lucas for more support.

Lucas waves them forward.

"You three are all Valkyrie's? How is it that I can sense and see this from Alex but not from you two? Also, what else are you Alex besides a valkyrie?" Eric finishes asking these questions but I don't know how to answer them.

People aren't supposed to know what we are or who I am.

ACKNOWLEDGMENTS

Thank you, to my parents Stephen and Amy. Having you in my corner is something I treasure. No matter what you are always there.

My wonderful editor Katelyn. We have grown closer over this past year and am grateful for you. To have a friend not just be willing to read but go through what my mind comes up with brings me to happy tears.

Nicole and Corin are my wonderful sisters who were my testers outside of my editor. It brought me to a roaring laughter one morning when Nicole texted me. She swore at me for leaving you guys with a cliffhanger and for not having the second book finished yet. From there it has been her mission to get her hands on it.

ABOUT THE AUTHOR

B ree Knight comes from a family of creative and imaginative people. She has a Bachelor's in Fine Arts from North Dakota State University with an emphasis in Stained Glass art. She grew up an avid reader which led her to her love of fantasy fiction books and that creativity can be seen in her artwork.

Growing up the local library was one of the places that she would go with her sisters during the Minnesota summers on their bikes. It was a great place to get out of the heat and explore. At the library, her imagination was let loose into the pages of those books. She's held on to her love of reading to this day.

During the pandemic, she felt a need for a new creative outlet...writing. From there she started to create a world of her own with the characters resembling those in her life. To have this outlet and the backing of her family has been amazing.